Meet Me in a Taxi

Earl Diemel

DORRANCE PUBLISHING CO., INC.
PITTSBURGH, PENNSYLVANIA 15222

ISBN #0-8059-4152-5
Printed in the United States of America

First Printing

For information or to order additional books, please write:
Dorrance Publishing Co., Inc.
643 Smithfield Street
Pittsburgh, Pennsylvania 15222
U.S.A.

I was born at about 11 P.M. on December 25, 1924, on County Road T about one-and-a-half miles from Summit Lake, Wisconsin, in a two-room log cabin. My six older sisters and Ma and Pa were happy to have a brother that night. My pa was so happy that he lay a single-shot .22 by my side and said that was my Christmas present. Another sister came along about two years later. At that time my pa was running a logging camp.

When the depression hit, we moved to town. There were no jobs to support all of us kids, so he started making moonshine. I don't remember any other moonshine still that far out of town, so in the spring of 1931, Pa built one closer to town. It had good spring water, which makes pretty tasty moonshine. I loved to walk with my pa through the woods to the still. There were oak trees, lots of squirrels, hardwood, birch, etc. There was this one grove of Norway pine where, every once in a while, we would see a bobcat. The first time I saw the bobcat, I thought it was going to jump on us, but Pa assured me there was no danger. After that I was always looking for that bobcat. We would also see deer every now and then.

Many people said my pa's moonshine was good. He even delivered to the sheriff and a judge in Antigo. When the trade was slow in the local area, he had a judge connection in Oshkosh, Wisconsin. But all he wanted to do was have enough money to keep us from starving, so when some Chicago peddlers offered, he turned them down.

He had a 1928 Hudson with a big trunk in the back. In those days, it was still a good running vehicle. One day my pa shot a wolf. He knew he could get a twenty dollar bounty for it, so he tied the wolf over the back of the trunk, since the trunk was full of moonshine. To get the bounty, he had to take the wolf to Antigo. When we got there, we saw the sheriff and the deputy walking on the sidewalk. Pa stopped and showed the sheriff the wolf. Pa then said something else to the sheriff. The deputy guessed there was something else going on, so he asked my pa, "What's in the trunk?"

My pa said, "It ain't none of your damn business."

The sheriff looked at the deputy and agreed, "That's right, it ain't none of your damn business." Pa got the bounty money, then met the sheriff later to get rid of the moonshine. We got some more corn and sugar and headed home.

All that summer, everything was going smoothly. It was my job to scrape down the mash with a scraper and hand it out to my pa. He used three rotating mash boxes, each about five foot square: one was for working the mash, one was for draining, while one was airing out. My pa would lower me into the boxes with my shoes off and hand me a scraper to scrape it down. He gave me a bucket with which I filled the scrapings. By the time I got through and he lifted me out, I would be staggering from smelling the fumes. But it was fun, too, because where we dumped the mash, the squirrels, birds, and chipmunks would become very friendly.

That fall, someone squealed on my pa and the Feds came directly to his still. Someone came to tell Pa that the Feds were wrecking the still. Pa said, "Son, let's take a ride." We got in the car and drove about one-and-a-half miles to the still. Passing by the gravel pit, Pa noticed Pete and some of his boys loading gravel. They were using a team of horses and a wagon to haul the gravel. (Wagons for hauling gravel have loose planks on the wagon bunks and the ends of the planks are tapered, so when you wanted to dump the gravel, all you had to do was roll the plank, causing the gravel to fall though.) When we got to the still, there were three carloads of revenuers, some staying by the car while the rest tore up the still. My pa drove by them, went down the road, and came back. When he came back, they stopped him and asked what he was doing there and if he knew anything about a still. He said, "What still?" Then they asked him what he was doing out there. He said he was sort of new around there and that he was supposed to help Pete load gravel, but he must have missed the turn-off to the pit. So they took my pa in one of their cars while one of the Feds drove our car. The Fed tried asking me a few questions, but I wouldn't answer him. When we pulled into the gravel pit, and before they could get out to question Pete, my pa jumped out of the car, grabbed a shovel, and said, "Sorry I'm late, Pete."

Pete didn't know what was going on, but when the Feds came over and asked Pete, if this was the man supposed to help him load gravel, Pete looked at my pa and answered, "Yup." Well, that saved my pa that time.

About two weeks later on a weekend when there was a light snow lying on the ground, Pa said, "Let's go out to the still and see what we can salvage." Pa had hidden some small kegs of moonshine in the ditch and covered them with brush, and when the Feds went in to tear up the still, they never found them. Anyway, they did a great job of tearing things up.

While we were there Pa noticed some large bear tracks, so we followed them a little ways. Pa laughed and told me the was drunk. He showed me the erratic tracks and where the bear would fall against a tree, knocking the snow off the branches. He also told me that the bear would not be going very far in that condition. So we went back home, picked up a rifle and Pa's friend Otto with his rifle. (Even bear meat tastes good when there's nothing else to eat.) Well, we started tracking the bear, and it wasn't long before we saw where the bear fell down. By the impressions in the snow, he must have lain there for a while. About one-and-a-half hours later, we came upon the bear on an old logging road. My pa pulled up his old Remmington .35 and shot. The bear fell over, so we walked up to him. My pa poked the bear with rifle and said, "Pretty good-sized bear, huh, Otto?" About that time, the bear took a swipe with his paw and ripped my pa's pants leg open. He never touched the flesh, but my pa put a couple more slugs into his head real quick. We took the bear home to the woodshed and skinned him out. The meat was a little greasy, but not too bad.

Terry, my buddy, was adopted by some people who owned a little grocery store. One day we decided we wanted some candy, but not having any money, we decided to swipe a couple of candy bars. Not knowing the difference, he swiped a couple of chocolate Ex-lax. It was a good thing they had a two-hole outhouse and a big Sears catalog, because we sat there for the better part of a day, using up half of that catalog!

That same summer, I had a little toy red wrecker about five inches long. It was the only toy I had for quite a while. Then someone stole my wrecker. One day when I was over at Terry's house, I saw my little red wrecker. So, I stole it back! When I got home with my wrecker, my pa asked me where I had found it. I told him that Terry stole it, but I stole it back! He told me that stealing was not the thing to do, so my pa took me by the ear and made me take the little red wrecker back to Terry's. I even had to apologize for stealing my little red wrecker! Terry then said that it was mine anyway so I should keep it.

Pa also had jugs and kegs of moonshine hidden around the woodshed and in the woods by our home. There were loose boards on the bedroom floor where we would store moonshine, covering the floorboards with a rug. They knew it was my pa making and selling the moonshine, but they could not catch him making or selling it. There was some moonshine around the house most of the time. One day my ma was home alone when they came with a search warrant. There were two quart-jars of shine in the cupboard as well as some under the floor. Ma happened to see them drive up, so she took the two quarts and put them in the hot-water reservoir in the cookstove. They couldn't find a thing. My pa was really pleased about her quick thinking.

There was an old stump in the woods a little ways from the house where Pa hid a jug. One day Dale came over, and we decided we needed a drink. We couldn't hold the jug and drink, so we set the jug on the stump. We spilled some, but we also got some inside of us. When my ma saw us coming down the road, she realized where we had been, and she was mad. But she couldn't help laughing because one of us would fall down and the other would trip over him and then it would start all over again.

Another thing my younger sister and I would do is suck the hose they used to drain the moonshine out of the kegs. The fumes could make you pretty silly. Ma used to get mad at us for doing that, too.

Things were pretty slim that winter, the only moonshine Pa sold was what was hidden in the woods and in the floor. The next spring, he borrowed some money and bought a one-room cottage on Bass Lake. I think my two older sisters had left home by then. He built another room for the bedrooms. All we had for partitions were blankets hanging around the beds. He built another still on a creek between Summit Lake and Bass Lake. He dug a hole in the creek bed to hold the water for the dry summer months. He put a few logs around it so no one would fall in. The still was built on the same order as the last one which the Feds had torn up. Just about everyone in town knew it was there. He sold the moonshine for fifty cents a quart or one dollar a gallon. If someone wanted something better, my pa would tell me, "Son, go get them a sample of that keg that's been aging for a long time." We had the moonshine stored in the root cellar. I would go and draw some from the same keg that I had the first time. My pa would say that it was fifty cents or one dollar a gallon higher. They would taste and exclaim, "That's much better," and pay the extra. My pa would cut the moonshine down from 120 proof to 100 proof. To age and color it, he would take oak shavings and put them in the oven to brown, then put them in the keg of whiskey. It was more convenient to age the whiskey at the cottage than at the still. I wasn't big enough yet to carry a keg home, so I would put it in a wheelbarrow and wheel it home. Ma and I would put it on the wood heater in the bedroom portion of the cottage, add some wood chips and keep a low fire going. Pa got to be well-known for his good moonshine, and people started coming to the cottage to get it.

Living at the cottage, my younger sister and I decided to go over and see Tom Moore, a farmer who lived about three-quarters of a mile away. In order to get there, we had to cut through Jim M.'s farm. While going through his farm, we decided we needed a couple of "rudabeggy." So we dug up a couple of Jim's rudabeggy, and we cut the skin off with a pocket knife. We were chewing on them but decided they needed salt. Jim wasn't home, so we went in and borrowed his salt shaker. Where Jim saw us, we don't know, but when we got home that evening, we both got the strap.

While at the cottage, we saw my pa use a long stick with a cloth doused with kerosene wrapped around the end of it to burn down a hornet's nest. My sister and I found a hornet's nest off the road a little ways from the cottage. We decided to do what Pa did and burn the hornet's nest. The hornets got mad, making us drop the stick. It caught the woods on fire. Quite a few of the townspeople came with shovels and wet blankets to put out the fire. We got lucky that day!

Our cottage was one mile from town, and between our cottage and town were four hills, the first was the smallest, the next a little larger, until you got to the fourth hill, which was the largest and steepest. For fun one of my sisters and I would hitch a ride on the back bumper of the car of someone who had come to get moonshine, then get off when they got to the forth hill where the going got very real slow. One day, one of my older sisters and I hitched a ride on a Model T Ford. We were at the second hill, where the trail cut off to go to the still, when my pa suddenly came out of the woods and saw us. He yelled at us, and we fell off the car, got up, and started running with Pa chasing after us. My sister, Lil, was older than I, so she could run faster. Pa caught me. He cut off some blackberry briers and whipped my butt. I sat very carefully for the next couple of weeks. Ma had to pull some of the thorns out of my butt, but some had to fester out. That ended my hitching rides on other people's bumpers.

Summit Lake is the highest spring-fed lake in Wisconsin. It flows into Bass Lake then to Waterpower Lake, into Kettle Hole Lake, Deepwood Lake, and finally into Bougus Marsh. In the spring the fish would run between the lakes, mainly downstream, so the local people as well as other folks from towns further away would come and spear fish at night because it was against the law to spearfish. The conservation department didn't care much if the people would spear suckers because they were scavengers, but the northern pike and the bull heads would run at the same time, so the conservation department outlawed all spearfishing. I was too small to spear, but I could carry the gunnysacks and fill them with fish. When they got too heavy with fish, I would hide the gunnysack and start another one. I was with some guys from Antigo one night when the suckers were really running. A couple of guys were wading the creek in hip boots because the water was really cold. They would spear a fish and shake it off on my side of the creek. My pa went the other way off the road with some other guys. He warned the guys with me that when they got up by the still they need to be careful because there was a deep hole there. It was a dark night, and they were using strong flashlights to see the fish. I was picking up fish and putting them in the gunnysack when they came up by the still and saw the log across the creek. Not realizing they were that close to the still, this one guy stepped over the log. He did a somersault right into the hole my pa had dug. He let out a bloodcurdling yell, and came up spitting and sputtering. He crawled out of the creek. He was shivering so bad I think he shivered up a sweat. That ended the fishing for the night But they had plenty of fish anyway Suckers are a bony fish, but in the spring, the meat is firm and tastes really good smoked.

Where the creek went under the road to our cottage, there were two four-foot culverts. My pa made a three-foot by six-foot funnel-trap made out of chicken wire. The trap tapered down at the funnel end to about a six-inch hole, and when the fish went in the trap, they could not get back out. So we put the trap into one of the culverts and tied it to a tree. We could pull it out early in the morning. One morning I went alone because the fish weren't running much. When I pulled out the trap, there were a bunch of bullheads and one muskrat. I had to beat the hell out of the trap to kill the muskrat with a club. There were 160 bullheads in the trap, so we gave away fish to a lot of folks in town.

During the summer on Bass Lake we could generally catch enough fish for a meal. So that summer we ate well. With winter coming on, we kids had to walk a mile to school in Summit Lake. The fall was pretty with the trees changing colors, so it was an enjoyable walk to school. Coming back from school in the evening, the first half mile we could walk along a path on Summit Lake, then cut up through the cemetery to the road going to our cottage. The cemetery was located on a small hillside overlooking the lake with spruce trees scattered around. Two families lived where the road cut off the county road to the cottage. One had a small farm and the other just a home. Each family had boy my age. When we would walk home together from school, we would get into a fight. Sometimes both were against me and sometimes two of us against the other. It all depended on how we felt. Aldy lived on the farm and Kelly lived next door. Aldy had a police dog named Brownie and once in a while when I got past his place, he would sick Brownie on me, wanting him to bite me. But I would call, "Here Brownie, here Brownie," and the dog would come running toward me, and we would play for awhile having him chase a stick. Then I would tell Brownie to go home. When the dog got back home, Aldy would beat the dog for not biting me.

That winter the snow was deep, so our half-mile of road was snowed in. The county would not plow it because it was a private road. We would trudge through the snow to go to school. My pa had enough deer hung around in the woods to help the meat situation. (The deer would stay frozen all winter, so when we needed meat we just went out and sawed a piece off.) As spring approached, I guess Pa conned the county into opening our road. Their first try was with a four-wheel-drive truck and a V-plow, but they couldn't even make a dent off the county road onto our road. Then they brought out a Cat with a V-plow which got almost to the big hill. They had to bring out a larger Cat with a V-plow with "wings" (which open up higher on the plow) to push the snow out further so it wouldn't fall in behind. The snowbank after they opened the road was way above the cars and there was only one lane open. When the thaw started, the road became so muddy we walked up on the snow where the wings had pushed it out furthest. As the snow melted even more, a nice lake formed between the third and fourth hills. In fact, it got so deep that cars could not go through it. We would have to cut around the pond through the woods. Finally, the snow was melted down, the grass was greening the bare spots, and wild lilies grew along with violets and arbutuses (the Wisconsin flower.)

Prohibition on the way out, so Pa thought business would be pretty rough. Instead, it was better because the whiskey they sold over the bar was such rotgut that they kept buying my pa's whiskey because it was better and cheaper.

Pa bought me a new wagon. It was the best, dual wheels on the rear plus sideboards. I was so proud of that wagon. Our cottage had a fairly wide circular drive. I used to park my wagon at a angle next to the cottage and the woodshed. Where I parked it, it stuck a little bit out in the driveway. (I guess being so proud of it, I wanted everyone to see it.) My pa kept warning me that that was not the place to park it and told me to park it alongside the garage where it would not get hit. I would do that for a couple of days, but if I hauled some wood or moved a keg, it would be right back in the driveway. One day some guys came in and made a left turn in the circular drive. They probably did not see the wagon. When they hit it, they bent the rear axle and goofed up the wooden bed. I was madder than hell, and my pa didn't say a word because he knew I was so proud of that wagon. The next day he was cutting up an oak tree to age the whiskey. I was watching him use a one-man crosscut saw when he said, "Son, do you know how this tree was felled?"

I knew it was struck by lightning, but I said "No, and I don't give a damn either." That was the wrong thing to say. He pulled the end of the saw back with one hand and put pressure on the other. When he let go, it hit me across the butt bouncing me about five feet. I had teeth marks from that saw on me for a while! After a little discipline, I did not question my pa too much.

Another day there were some guys down to buy whiskey. They were sitting around sipping some and trying to make a deal. I don't know how the conversation started about drinking whiskey and worms, but my pa said, "Son, go out in the garden and dig out a couple of angle worms (or fish worms)." I didn't question my pa so I went out to the garden and dug up a couple of worms. When I came back in, he had a glass of whiskey and a glass of water sitting on the table. He said to me, "Now son, clean them off." (All you do is strip off the dirt). Then he told me to put one worm in the whiskey and one in the water, which I did. The worm in the whiskey just shriveled up and died. The one in the water just swam around. My pa said, "Son, now what does that teach you?" I said, "Pa, if you drink whiskey, you will never have worms!" (Maybe that's why I don't have worms today!)

In the town of Summit Lake, a tavern named Palace of Mirrors opened up, but as I said earlier, the moonshine was selling better than the government booze. One day when my pa and I were at the still, Mose G. came running through the woods. He said, "George, the Feds are coming to get you and tear up the still." We had just enough time to get away from the still and up on a little hill before they came, guns and all. There were six of them, and they tore things up as we hid on the hill and watched. The reason they tore up the still was Barney, the owner of the Palace of Mirrors, who squealed on my pa. Mose just happened to be sitting outside the Palace of Mirrors when they were getting directions to where the still was, so Mose took off on the run through the woods to warn us. That's when my pa decided to go into competition with the Palace of Mirrors.

Pa opened a tavern, called Diemel's Tavern. He had to borrow some money from Vern (a friend of his). We had Miller High Life on tap, five cents for an eight-ounce glass and fifteen cents for a twenty-four-ounce chilled mug. The whiskey went for ten cents a shot for Ten High Whiskey and up to twenty-five cents a shot for Old Grandpa or the like. We had canned sardines with crackers or pickled herring to with the beer. The lumberjacks ate quite a bit of it.

My job was to keep the fires going. We had a large woodshed. In the fall we would get edgings from the sawmill and cut them up to stove length with a buzz saw. (Edgings are the part they cut off boards, the part that still has the bark on it.) The edgings were mainly for the kitchen stove. We would buy chunk wood by the truckload for the other three stoves.

After the first year of three wood-burning stoves and one kitchen stove, my pa decided to get modern. The two oil burners he got made a little less work, and the fires would go all night. I would have to clean the carburetors so the oil burners would keep going without clogging up. I got pretty good at doing that, I could take one apart and put it back together in about fifteen minutes!

We also had an icehouse in back. In the winter they would keep a large area of the lake cleared of snow. When the ice got to about the thickness of approximately eighteen inches, they would cut it up and put it in the icehouse. They packed the ice with sawdust from the sawmill. During the summer, until I got big enough to handle a full block of ice, my pa would pull it out of the icehouse and drop it to the ground. It was then my job to clean it off, chip it, and bring it into the bar to keep the beer, pop, and glasses cool. In the winter we would pump water into a couple of buckets or let it run on the ground, let it freeze, and then chop it up with an axe.

I think it was during the first year in the tavern, on a night when my pa and Tony (a good old lumberjack) were in the bar shooting the bull when a car drove up. Five guys walked in all dressed in suits, a sight you don't normally see up in the backwoods of Wisconsin, especially at 9:30 at night in the winter. They asked my pa if there was a wrecker in town. Pa said, "Sure." My pa got me out of bed and told me to go get Soupy, the town garage owner. They had run their car into a ditch about half a mile down the road. I put on warm clothes, and went with Soupy to pull them out. (My pa was afraid to leave the tavern because they looked pretty mean.) When we got to the car, there was one man waiting there. After Soupy pulled the car out, we went back to the tavern. They asked him how much he charged to pull the car out, and Soupy said, "Five bucks." They said, "Here's twenty dollars for your trouble." Then they lay twenty dollars on the bar for my pa and said,

"This is for your trouble." Although we didn't realize it then,, the was Dillinger who had a place not far from Summit Lake. Looking back, we should have recognized the signs of the Chicago-type Mafia cars, clothing, etc.

My sister, Marge, got tied up with a guy also named Earl. Good-looking guy, but wasn't too much for work. She was married and pregnant, but I don't know which came first. Wasn't long after they were married that he held up a service station and got caught. Marge got a divorce and came home. She had a son named Ron.

In the meantime, Ray, a trapper, killed a female coyote that had four pups. I liked Ray and I guess he liked me, because he saved one of the pups for me. He killed the rest and got a twenty-dollar bounty on each one. I named my new pet Wolfe. We also made a sandpit for Ron to play in. Since he wasn't old enough to walk yet, he stayed put. We had Wolfe on a chain (he would chew a rope in two), but he guarded Ron so well that when it was time to take Ron in, the only two people that could pick him up were my mother and myself. Marge could not pick up her own son without being barked or snapped at.

We also had a sow pig fenced in part of the backyard, which we would butcher in the fall. The way we cooled tap beer at that time was through copper tubes running through ice. In the morning, Pa, Ma, or I would have to run off a couple quarts of beer before we could serve. Once a week a guy would come through town with his steam cleaner and clean the coils. My pa got the idea instead to throw the beer to the sow instead of throwing it out. The old sow liked the beer so much that my pa had a special mug just for the pig. Every time Pa or anyone would take a glass of beer out, the old pig would come over, sit on her butt and drink the beer. The tourists would get such a kick out of that, they would start buying beer trying to get the pig drunk. After the pig got drunk she would try to walk, falling against the fence and almost breaking it. She would stagger around for a while, then sleep it off.

Of course, we would feed the pig corn plus leftovers. Our next-door neighbors owned a store and also had chickens, about sixty or seventy of them. They would let them run loose. We would tell Mrs. Percy, the neighbor, to keep the chickens out of the pigpen because they ate all the corn. Since the chickens had to hunt for most of their food, they thought the corn was pretty easy pickings. My pa told me to string a wire across the pigpen and hook Wolfe's chain to it. The little coyote would lay on top of the pigshed, until enough chickens began feeding, then he would come off the shed and start snapping chicken necks. So, we had lots of free chicken dinners, since he would get up to four every time they came into the pigpen. Mrs. Percy couldn't figure out how her chickens were disappearing and told my ma and pa about it. They just explained that if she would keep the chickens out of the pigpen, they would not disappear, but she didn't pay any attention to the advice. We were beginning to feel guilty about eating her chickens, because she was nice even if she was a tightwad. So we didn't put Wolfe in the pigpen for a while. Then the chickens started coming in regularly, but Wolfe played it cool. He lay onto the pigshed until they were feeding. Then he jumped down and started snapping necks. He got fourteen chickens that time, so Ma and I got the water boiling and cleaned the chickens. My pa took seven over to Mrs. Percy's store and said, "Here are some of your chickens, now please keep them out of the pigpen." It was the last time the chickens came over!

I had Wolfe for about three years, and we used to keep her chained up outside by the outhouse. People going by would see her and want to pet her. If they asked my pa he would tell them not to try. It would upset them sometimes because they could see me playing and wrestling with her. One guy didn't listen and got bit. My pa said I would have to get rid of her because we could not afford to get sued. I didn't have the heart to kill her and get the bounty, so I gave her to a friend in Antigo. She got away from him and was hanging around a slaughterhouse because they were feeding her. She got pregnant by a black lab and had five pups. After she had the pups, they killed her and the five pups for the got $120 bounty.

Besides keeping the fire going, getting ice, and pumping water, I also had to clean the spittoons. I hated those stinking S.O.B.'s. We had five of them because quite a few of the lumberjacks chewed tobacco or had snuff. My pa hardly ever gave me any money unless I earned it somehow. He would give money to a stranger in need before he gave his kids any. One day he asked me if I ever found money in the spittoon, and I answered that once in a great while I did. He knew how much I hated cleaning those spittoons, so I was surprised and grateful when I caught my pa walking by and dropping a dime or a quarter into one of them.

In the spring after the snow was gone, all the winter garbage stacked behind the houses had to be hauled to the dump. Mickey and I would charge families twenty-five or fifty cents to haul their winter garbage to the dump. With my wagon, it might take four or five trips.

When the spring plowing started, I would follow behind the plow picking up angle worms. I made a box out of old lumber in which to keep the worms. Then in the late summer when worms were hard to find I would sell them by the can for fifteen cents. Sometimes they even gave me extra because there were so many worms in each can.

Our school had two rooms, first to fourth grade in one room and fifth to eighth grade in the other. Our class was the largest at the time with eight boys and one girl. When I started school, I was left-handed. I guess that was a bad omen because my teacher tied my left hand down by my side so I would learn to write right-handed. (I still bat and throw left-handed.)

Going through school was pretty routine until the last two years of school when we got a male teacher. The female teacher we had before could not quite handle things. For example, it was in the spring that Mickey and I would take blackjack gum and put it on our teeth to make it look like our teeth were missing. Then we would look at the younger kids, smile, and get them laughing so hard they couldn't study. The teacher could not figure it out because there wasn't any whispering going on. When she caught us a few days later, the three of us (Dale had joined us) got suspended for two weeks. Dale's mother was on the school board so he got to go back. After he went back, they said we could go back, also. But we said we had been suspended for two weeks and were going to take it. We would make it a point when school was out for morning recess to go by with a can of worms and our fishing poles, heading for one of the lakes around. In the spring when the ice melts, fishing is pretty good.

Another example of the trouble we got into was we would stick our feet out in the aisles and trip the kids. The teacher would then stand in the back of the room with a pointer, and when she saw us stick our legs out, she would come by and hit our legs with it. Mickey and I wised up and got a little hand mirror. We would be watching through our hand mirror, and when she came up to hit us, we would pull our legs in. Instead of our legs, she would hit the steel on the desk with the pointer and sting her fingers.

After we got our male teacher, things were different. He started a basketball team in the basement. The ceilings were only eight feet high, so the basket was pretty low, but we had a lot of fun anyhow. We would go to other towns who were also small, but I don't remember ever winning a game. That spring before school was out, they had a P.T.A. meeting with all the mothers. For us to show our progress, we had to make up a poem that rhymed. When it came to my turn, I got up and said, "There was a lady named Miss Grass/She waded in the water up to her ankles." The teacher looked at me and said, "That doesn't rhyme,"

I said, "It would if the water were deeper." My mother got up and left, but the teacher told me to stay after school. Of course, the kids were laughing while their mothers were trying to keep a straight face. After school, the teacher and I were the only ones there. Instead of scolding me, he started to laugh. He explained that there is a time and place for jokes like that, and it wasn't in school. The next year, my last year at this school, was rather routine.

That summer, Mickey and I found a hornets' nest on a path down by the lake. We got to wondering what a hornets' nest looked like inside. After talking it over, we found some heavy gloves and put a gunnysack over our heads with the eyes and nose cut out so we could breathe and see. We proceeded to tear down the hornets' nest. Its a good thing there was a lake nearby, because those hornets were inside the gunnysacks so fast it wasn't even funny. We ran for the lake, pulling the gloves and sack off before diving into the water. Every time we came up for air, the hornets would be there. Finally, we swam underwater far enough to get away from them. When we got to shore, we had to hold our eyes open with our fingers to see our way home. That was the last time we tried to get in a hornets' nest. We were both sore for quite a while!

Spearing suckers and northern pike in the spring was a ritual, but one year Aldy, Dale B., Kelly L., and I decided to build a little dam and put a box trap in it. I think we got the idea in school because that was the way the Indians used to do it.

By cutting some green trees and rolling rocks off a side hill, we made the dam. We laid poles across the creek in back of it so we could walk on there and to support the trap. The box trap was about 3 feet by 5 feet with 1 by 10 chicken wire on the bottom. We had it rigged so if someone came, we could lift it out and carry it up into the woods. It was easy to hear someone in the quiet of night. We could get all the fish we could carry in a gunnysack in no time at all when they were running good. Some nights, it would take a little longer.

Well, the game warden could never catch us. And we knew the woods pretty well. In fact, we even had a little shack built away from the creek where we would wait while the trap was in. Every half-hour or so, we would sneak down and empty it.

One day (in daylight), the game warden and one of his stoolies came down to tear out our dam. They carried picks and shovels. (Dale B, Aldy, and I were across the creek in the woods watching.) Well, this stoolie tried to make a big showing. He took a big swing with the pick. It stung his hands so bad he almost dropped the pick. They tried a few more times before they left. The next day they came with some dynamite and blew it up.

When we found out what happened, we got some help and rebuilt the dam. It didn't take long after school to roll more rocks off the hillside.

We would also harass the game warden when he was down at the creek at night trying to catch someone spearing fish. A couple of us would act like we were spearing fish (most of us had strong flashlights in order to see in the water). Someone would yell "I got one." Maybe someone else would say something. Then we would get the game warden to chase us. We had trip wires tied between trees. We knew which ones you had jump over so they would trip the game warden. It got to the point that they did more sneaking than chasing. We never did get caught, even though quite a few other people did.

That same summer while I was swimming along the shore, I came upon a two-year-old girl drifting face-down in the water. I grabbed her, but she was turning blue already. I brought her to shore, laid her on a blanket face-down, and started pressing water out of her. I had revived her by the time her parents came over. They were very thankful.

Another time that same year, we took a trip down the Eau Claire Dells. It was a nice place with a roped-off pool, a trapeze set out over the river, big flat rocks surrounded by tables and chairs and two lifeguards on duty. My sister and I were out on the trapeze, swinging and diving into the deeper water. The lifeguards were watching us because we were so small. For some reason, I came into shore and was walking along on the flat rocks where kids playing. Their folks were sitting around drinking beer and pop. There was a good two-foot drop-off to the water, and just as I walked by a little girl fell into the river. I dove in and got her before she had a chance to go under. Even the lifeguards thanked me.

Going to high school, we had to catch a bus at Kay's grocery store, which was on the north end of town. Kay sold out to a guy named Emil. He was one of the tightest persons around. One day while waiting for the school bus, I went in and bought a bottle of pop. When he gave me the pop, I asked if I could have a straw. He said to me, "Do you realize those straws cost a penny a piece?"

I said "Bullshit, they cost eighty cents a box, and the box has 500 straws in it." I explained to him that I know what things cost because I ordered them lots of times at home.

Emil said "Get out of my store," and came around the counter to kick me out. Around this time, Pepsi came out with bottled six-packs. He had them stacked just as you came into the store. When he went to kick me in the butt as I was leaving the store, his leg came up and I reached out and simply pulled up on his leg. Emil was tall and lanky, so when he fell over backward, he knocked over his Pepsi stack, and broke a bunch of bottles. Instead of leaving, I ran back into the store. I don't know why I did it, but when he was trying to get up, he reached out and tried to take a swing at me with his fist. He missed and put his fist through a glass candy showcase. Then I jumped over the Pepsi bottles and left. The other kids outside asked what had happened, so I told them. They thought it was pretty funny because none of them liked Emil. The bus was should have been about there, but I thought I'd best tell my pa before someone else did. He said he thought it was sort of funny, but that maybe he had better go to the store to get something and see if Emil had anything to say. When Pa walked into the store, Emil was cleaning up the mess. He didn't say anything. Emil didn't last long in Summit Lake, only about a year and a half.

On Halloween night, Mickey and I were walking around thinking of what we should do. We stopped by the garage, shot the bull a little, bought a candy bar, and left. It wasn't very late yet, only a little after 9:00 P.M. Mickey said he didn't feel too good, and I told him that I wasn't in the mood for halloweening either, so we both went home. I went to bed. At 11:00 P.M. my pa and some other town people woke me up and started asking me questions about what we did that night. I told them truthfully not much of anything. They asked if we ate any candy, and I told them that we had bought a candy bar at the garage. I finally asked what was wrong, and they told me Mickey was dead. It was hard for me to believe. They performed an autopsy and found out that he only had half a heart. It sure was a shock because we were such good buddies.

Wayne R. was pretty much a mama's boy whose folks had a service station about two blocks from downtown. Wayne could never go out on Halloween, but this one year his mother said he could go if he went with me. The first thing we decided to do was tip over Soupy's outhouse, the one behind the garage downtown. It was really cold that night, and Soupy had it anchored pretty well. There were four or five of us all pushing. It finally went over, but Wayne fell in. We pulled him out. His pant legs froze, and he headed for home walking with legs spread and arms bobbing. We felt sorry for him, but we couldn't help laughing. It was the only time he was allowed to go out on Halloween.

That winter the Chicago Northwestern Railroad contracted our town to cut ice for the railroad. The cakes had to be thirty-six inches deep, thirty-six inches long, and twelve inches wide. They used the county grader to keep the snow off the ice so it would freeze faster. Soupy made an ice saw from a car motor and a buzz saw. it even had a guide to cut the right width. The saw was on skids. It was a big deal for the people in town because it gave the people who did not work in the woods a chance to make some extra money by helping load the ice in boxcars. From there they would take the loaded ice to a storage shed in Antigo. My pa pulled the chunks out of the lake and onto the ice. When I wasn't in school, I would do the same. We had corks on our boots so we would not slip and so we could notch the ice. To get the ice out of the water, you would catch it with ice tongs, get a good bite on the cake of ice, pulling it up a little way. Then you would shove it down in the water as far as you could. The ice would push up to float on the top of the water, so you would have to give a hard yank and pull it out of the water. These blocks were really heavy because they were so large.

We would also help load the sleighs. The farmers used their teams and a couple of pickup trucks but the trucks could not haul as much. We got two cents a cake for loading, and they got four cents a cake for hauling. I don't remember what Soupy got for cutting.

One day when my pa and I were walking home for lunch, we walked by Emil's store. Emil had a Spitz dog that was sort of mean. The dog came out from under the back porch and tried to bite my pa on the leg. But when he got close, my pa swung and kicked him with the corks on his boots. It peeled the dog's nose back. The dog went back under the porch and died. We felt sorry for the dog. Emil came up to the tavern that night and asked my pa why he had kicked his dog. My pa said "What was I supposed to do as the dog came up and was going to kick me first." Emil stormed out of the tavern, and that was the end of that. He sold the store the next summer.

While going to high school in Elcho, I wasn't too happy. The boys from Elcho didn't like the newcomers from Summit Lake flirting with their girls. So after one year of going to Elcho, I decided I wasn't going back.

In the winter the Faith brothers would cut cedar post. In the spring they would peel the bark off and sell the posts according to size to farmers in southcentral Wisconsin and Iowa. The reason they would cut them in the winter and haul them to a landing site near town is because a cedar swamp is too wet in the summer. In the winter it would freeze over, making hauling easier. The Faith brothers were paying two cents a post to peel them, so I decided that would be a good way to make extra money. They said I could peel post, and since I was a fourteen-year-old greenhorn, they gave me a pile of dry cedar post. (When cedar is dry, there is no sap in the tree, and you have to dry-shave all the way to get the bark off. With the green cedar post, all you have to do is start a strip, snap it, and it peels off the length of the post.) The old experts could peel 100 posts a day and then go home or to the tavern for a beer. They were leaving around 3:30 P.M. for the day, yet I was still working my butt off trying to get 100 posts done. Sometimes I would have to work till 6:30 or 7:00 P.M. to make a 100. It took me about four days to realize I had been screwed! Peeling posts lasted about two weeks, then they were hauled to southern Wisconsin.

When Pa went into the tavern business, he sold the 1929 Hudson he had. We didn't have a car for about five years until he bought a 1929 Dodge, four-door touring sedan. It would start in the coldest winter when nothing else around town would start.

Anyway, one day in the spring Pa and I were going fishing at Waterpower Lake. We just got out of town a little way to where the road was washed out from the spring thaw. I was driving, and Pa told me to straddle the ditch which was full of water. We just went a little way before the bottom dropped out. There sat the old Dodge on its running boards. Pa got out and said, "It looks like you're stuck. We'll see you when you get out." He then walked home.

I was wondering how to get the car out when I remembered Bill W. had brought his Cat out to the woods. Bill was gone, but I knew he wouldn't care if I used it. So I walked through town, saw Dale B., and asked him to drive the car. He said that he didn't know how. I told him all he had to do was steer it. So we went and fired up the Cat and got the car out. All Pa said to me was, "I knew you would figure out something."

Another time Pa and I went to float the Hunting River. We had to drive about twelve miles to get there. We had a flat-bottomed boat about 16 feet long which we carried on the top of the car. The fishing was good and the water was low, so in some of the ripples, we would have to get out and pull the boat across. We had already gotten three northern pike and two trout when we came upon another ripple. My pa said, "That's enough of this." He got out and headed into the woods and said to me, "See you when you get home." (The way the river ran it was about three miles from home at that point.) I had to row upstream quite awhile. It took me about four hours to get to the car. When I got to the car it was almost 9 P.M. and by the time I dragged the boat to the car and got it loaded, it was 11:00 P.M. I got home at 11:30 and walked in the tavern. My pa only said, "Well I see you made it."

Being fourteen years old and swimming in the lake all summer, I was tanned like an Indian. The little town of Summit Lake was a tourist town in the summer because of the good swimming and fishing. This one married couple came up to stay in a cottage for a few weeks. She was eighteen and he was twenty-six, and they were just married. I don't know why, but she was turned on to me. The first time I realized something was up was when she came to Summit Lake alone and stayed with us at the tavern. In the morning when I was going down the stairs, I passed by her room. She said, "Hi Earl," and threw the bed covers off. She was naked. I was only fourteen and bashful, and she was married, so I just said hi and kept on going. In the meantime, I learned to drive a truck in the woods. Besides selling my fish worms, the Olden brothers would pay me twenty-five cents a load to drive for them in the woods. They were hauling hemlock bark, and with me driving, they did not have to jump in and out of the truck. They would haul a load of bark to the freight cars and load the freight cars with the bark, after which the railroad would take it to the southern part of the state. The bark was for tanning deer and cattle hides. We would haul three to four loads a day, which was fairly good money not counting my learning to drive.

That fall I went to southern Wisconsin to drive truck during peapack (hauling peas from the field to the canner). I stayed with a couple that had just been married. Her husband would have to work late at night because they owned a tavern. She would come home early to tuck me in. We both enjoyed it, so it became a nightly ritual. The hours were long driving a truck, but the pay was good, about twenty dollars a day.

After my one year of high school in Elcho, I didn't care to go back, so for the next two years, I worked in the woods, drove logging trucks and helped in the tavern.

In 1941, I started high school in Antigo. We would ride a bus from Summit Lake to Antigo. That way I would be home every night. On December 7, 1941, I was sitting in the living room listening to the radio. They announced that Japan had bombed Pearl Harbor. I went into the tavern and told everyone there about the bombing of Pearl Harbor. They all gathered around the radio to listen. Radio reception in northern Wisconsin isn't great, but our Cornodo radio was one of the best in town. Other townspeople started to gather at our house to hear the broadcast.

After only half a year of high school, I decided to quit. I took an NYA (National Youth Administration) course, an aviation course. Also, I cleaned the two movie theaters in Antigo. The pay wasn't great, but I got into the movies free as well as taking the NYA course. I met this gal named Elaine. When Margie and her husband went out, I would baby-sit their son, Ron. Elaine would come over and help me baby-sit. One evening I noticed I was getting a little peach fuzz under my nose. Elaine was coming over that evening so to make my peach fuzz look more like a mustache, I took my sister's eyebrow pencil and darkened it. We were kissing pretty heavily, and when I came up for air, I noticed that Elaine had a mustache, too! I bet when she went home that night and looked in the mirror, she was surprised!

Another night, I was supposed to meet Betty M. to take her to the movie. I was to meet her on a corner about two blocks past Elaine's house. As I was walking by Elaine's, Elaine walked out the door. She said, "I have to go to the library. I can walk with you." I couldn't tell Elaine no, because I was going out with her fairly regularly, so when we came to Betty M. on the corner, I asked Betty M. if she were going somewhere. In a very disgusted voice she said, "I was until now!" Betty was really a cute gal, and I would have liked to date her, but that was the end of that!

After finishing my aviation course, I was still too young to go in the service, being only seventeen. So I joined the CCC (Civilian Conservation Corps) instead. I was a truck driver there. They didn't have too many seventeen-year-olds that even knew how to drive. They were closing up the CCC because of the war, and after transferring to two other camps, I ended up in Hixton, Wisconsin. I picked up a couple of girlfriends at Black River Falls, thirteen miles from Hixton, and I had to hitchhike to get there. Local people were always willing to give a guy in uniform a ride. We were always supposed to be back at camp by the eleven o'clock curfew. One night I was with Marlea when it got to be later than I thought, so I waited until morning to hitchhike back. Imagine my surprise when it was our commanding officer who picked me up. The first thing he said was, "When you get back to camp, you had better change your pants." I looked down, and my suntans had some bloodstains on them. (I guess it was the wrong time of the month.) He didn't say much else to me about curfew since my brother-in-law was another officer at the camp.

At Hixton I was on contour-plowing for planting trees. I would go to the farm with a transit and shoot grades for them to plow for contour-planting. That lasted awhile, until they put me in an office in the courthouse for soil testing. That was also a pretty good job. Sometimes the girls would even come down to visit me.

At Black River Falls, near the river, there was a place they called "the Rock." To get to the Rock, you had to go through a cemetery to the shore and jump about five feet out into the river onto the rock. That was a regular lovemaking place. Late one afternoon, Marlea called me and asked me to come over because a tornado had just come through town. I hitchhiked over to town and while walking to her home, I stumbled over something on the curb. I looked down and saw it was the top side of a street sign that had been driven into the ground. After looking at all the houses that had been damaged, we decided to go out on the Rock. That night after the storm, it got pitch black. We were trying to feel our way through the cemetery. All of a sudden, she fell away from me and let out a big scream. Not knowing what had happened or where she was, I got out my cigarette lighter. There was

Marlea, lying on a coffin. A tree had blown over and uprooted the coffin. Needless to say, there was no necking that night!

The pay at the CCC was thirty dollars a month, they gave me thirteen dollars and sent the rest home. My folks saved the money for me. I joined a of couple squad leaders in loaning out our money for 100 percent interest back on payday. We were doing a good business! About once a month, we hired a cab to go to the whorehouses in Wionia, Minnesota. We always took one of our better cash customers with us. I wasn't old enough to go into the bar then, so a friend would let me use his driver's license as my ID. My name changed to Herman Schwartz for a night. After five months of working with the CCC the folks wanted me to come home and help in the tavern. So I went home, but that didn't last long either, because I was impatient to join in the war. Boeing Aircraft in Seattle were looking for employees with aviation experience. They paid our way to Seattle, to work at the aircraft factory. Five of us went there to work. We took the Northern Pacific Railroad and it was the first time in my life that I saw the mountains. They were was really beautiful with all the snow. We even got to see an avalanche. We had to wait for six hours before they cleared the tracks. I didn't care because the mountains were so beautiful. When we got to Seattle, it was raining. The three days we waited for an interview, it rained all the time. We decided to leave and check on work in Portland, Oregon. We took a bus to Portland, but it was still raining. We got so tired of the rain that we didn't even stop in Portland. We just kept going until we reached San Francisco, but even there it was still raining! Two of the guys said "To hell with this," and decided to go back home. Three of us continued down to Los Angeles. Finally, it wasn't raining anymore. It was now about a month before Christmas. We checked with several different companies, but no one was hiring before the first of the year.

Someone suggested we check with Sears and Roebuck. Sears said they could use two of us. We drew straws, and Houser and I went to work. We made up orders for shipping. I ran out of money and had to wire home for fifty dollars until I got paid. Because it was Christmas, shipping was slowing down. They were going to lay us off, but one of the supervisors told me I could come back at the first of the year to start working again. So we stayed at a hotel right downtown.

It was Christmas Eve and my birthday was Christmas Day, so we found a guy, explained our situation, and gave him money to buy a quart of whiskey for us. Sipping on the bottle, we decided to go to a movie. At the movie, we got to feeling a bit rowdy and they threw us out. Houser was so drunk I had to hold him by the back of his jacket to keep him from falling. Going through the park to get to our hotel, Houser got sick. He just sat on a park bench leaning over being sick. A queer came up and sat down beside me. He put his hand on my knee and said "Your buddy's kinda sick, isn't he?" I turned to him and said, "Yep," and threw up all over him. Nobody bothered us anymore that night!

A couple days later, Houser decided to go back to Wisconsin. I went out and applied for a job at North American Aviation in El Segundo, Califonia. They told me to report for employment on January 3. My aviation course didn't mean a thing to them because they put me on cadmium plating of certain parts. After turning eighteen on Christmas, I had to sign up for the draft. While I stayed in Los Angeles I would catch a bus, go to the pier in Ocean Park, and listen to the big bands. Glen Miller, Tommy Dorsey, and Gene Krupa were some of the bands I listened and danced to. When you went in, you bought tickets for ten cents a dance. Then you would ask a girl to dance and give her a ticket. I wasn't a good dancer, so sometimes I would just sit with the girl. I enjoyed that. One of my sisters was living in Venice then, and I had dinner with her and her family on some Sundays.

The draft was getting closer to calling my name, so North American said they could get me a deferment if I wanted them to. I said no because all my buddies were going in, and I didn't think it would be right. In the latter part of February, I bought a bus ticket to northern Wisconsin. The bus took the southern route through Texas then headed north. Leaving Los Angeles, I met this gal headed to Kansas City. We started doing a little kissing on the bus (it was dark and there weren't too many people on the bus). We decided to go to the back seat, which was all the way across the back. We got pretty hot, so every now and then the bus driver would turn on the light to check on us. After two days together on the bus, she started acting serious, so I told her if she wanted me, she would have to come second because the army had me first. We split up in Kansas City, and I continued on to Chicago, where I had to change buses. I had just summer clothes on coming from Los Angeles, and with the wind coming off Lake Michigan, I just about froze to death. When I got to Antigo and I reported to the draft board. They said I would probably be called in a month. A friend of mine who had two kids was being called, and I asked if I could take his place so he could have a little more time at home. On March 11, 1943, I was called to board a train in Antigo to go to Fort Sheridan, Illinois. Two days before that, the taverns were giving us all free drinks, so we were really celebrating. Our girlfriends didn't want to see us go, but duty comes first. The day we boarded, my pa gave me two pints of whiskey. I put them in my jacket pockets. The girls all lined up on the station platform to kiss us goodbye, and it was cold. When we got in the passenger's coach, it was really warm in there. So warm, in fact, that one of the guys threw up in the aisle, making us all sick from the smell and heat. The toilets were locked because we were at the station, so I knocked out a window on the opposite side of the station where several of us lost our cookies. After we got underway, it got much colder with the window out, so they made me sit by the window since I had knocked it out. The porter gave each of us a pillow, but my pillow went right to the window! The next morning we stayed in a hotel. On March 14, 1943, we were inducted into the service. The two pints of whiskey my pa had given me were still full. A sergeant at Fort Sheridan checking us saw those two pints and said I couldn't keep them. I asked him what he was going to do with them, and he said he would pour them down the sink. I thought for a second and said, "If that's the case, let me take them and pour them down the sink." He asked me if I didn't trust him, and I said "Sure, but this way, if I can't have them, nobody else can either." (I think I broke his heart.) The Marines were looking for top physically fit inductees. But I had made a deal with Butch Olsen that we would both take the Army. Butch turned chicken on me and took the Navy. I ended up in the Army in Fort Warren in Cheyenne, Wyoming, for basic training. There were quite a few guys from the eastern states, and some of them had never been away from home. The wind in Cheyenne blows pretty hard that time of year. We had to drill on a drill field made of decomposed granite (small stones). Marching, we had to lean into the wind, and the small stones would hit us in the face. The drill field was also near Crow Creek. With close-order drill, the sergeant would make a point of saying "When I say march you march." The platoon would be marching when the sergeant yelled, "Rear hatch." But some of us would just keep marching toward the creek as if we couldn't hear his command. The sergeant would then come running, waving his hands, and hollering "Halt, halt." We would have to fall out and re-assemble; it got to be a game. We would get weekend passes to go into Cheyenne. One of the favorite spots was the roller rink or the USO. Generally, four or five of us guys went. The girls in Cheyenne were friendly, so it wasn't hard to get a date or a little loving. Some of my buddies could not get the girls to go all the way, they asked me how I did it. I didn't really know. The girls were friendly, and they liked my company, I guess. They bet five dollars that I could not go all the way with one of their girls, so I bet them that I could. After I told them all the action, they paid me five dollars, but then they got to where they didn't believe me. So after that, I would have to come back to base with a stinky finger and let them smell. One night I was with Joyce. She was friends with three little sisters, and we all went to the roller rink together. Joyce introduced them to me as Muriel, the oldest, Lillian, and Zelda. Joyce lived over the railroad tracks, and the three sisters lived just off East Lincoln Highway in Cheyenne. I was going with Joyce, and we were visiting with Vera, who lived close to the railroad tracks, when Muriel came over with her boyfriend, Stan. Vera's folks traveled a lot, so all her girlfriends would bring their boyfriends over. One day, Stan decided he was going to make a play for Joyce. He talked Joyce into going in the bedroom, but they left the door open and were smooching on the bed.

I said to Muriel, "As long as they are doing that, we can do the same." So she and I went out on the porch and sat on the swing. While necking, I made a date to take her to the movies. Later, I walked Joyce home, gave her a good-bye kiss, and walked back to the base. The day of the date I went to Vera's to pick up Muriel. The reason Muriel and the three sisters went to

Vera's to meet their dates was because their folks did not want them dating servicemen. The folks were afraid the servicemen would get the girls in trouble and then leave. Stan didn't have a date, but he happened by Vera's that night.

He said, "Muriel's not going with you."

I replied, "I think she is."

Muriel said she was going.

Stan then said, "You will have to whip me first."

I said as I opened the door, "There's forty acres out here, so we better get started." Stan backed down. (Muriel and I went to the movie, but we were not really serious about each other. All Muriel wanted to do was neck.)

July 3, they shipped forty of us out. We didn't know where we were going, but they put us on a train sitting with civilians. We were headed south out of Cheyenne. The next morning, July 4, we were in Pueblo, Colorado. The train had to take on coal and water, so we had about a half-hour layover. I went into the store and bought about five dollars worth of fireworks to celebrate when we got off the train. When we got back to the train, a couple of WAC's got on. We reversed our seats to face them. I'm sitting there holding my fireworks between my legs, when one of the guys reached under the seat from the back and lit the sack. It was flaming pretty good before I realized it, so I threw it under the WAC's feet. When the firecrackers started going off, the gal jumped right over the top of the seat, cussing us out. After that, they wouldn't talk to us anymore. One guy brought a bale of hay on board. When another guy asked why he had brought the bale of hay, the first guy said to feed his nightmares. Bob and I were sitting next to one another when two other gals got on the train. There were no more seats available, and they said they were going to Kansas City. We told them if they wanted to sit down, they could sit down in our laps. They said okay. The one that sat on my lap was at least six feet tall with strawberry blond hair. We put our jackets over us, we all ended up having a good time smooching!

When we got into Kansas City, the gals wanted us to go AWOL for a few days, but we said no.

I think it was in St. Louis when we got a car of our own. It was a lounge car, and I guess you know we felt like we were in high heaven. The next time the train stopped for coal and water, we got off to get beer and whiskey. We still didn't know where we were going, but we were really enjoying ourselves, sitting there like big wheels and drinking beer and whiskey. On the third day, we arrived in Danville, Illinois, at about 1:30 in the afternoon. About a third of us were loaded. A captain came in the railroad car and asked us if we had had a good trip. We all answered, "Yes, sir." He saw all the beer and whiskey bottles sitting around us and he said, "It looks like you really did. But now, we are going to have to straighten up and look like soldiers, since we have to march right through downtown Danville. Tomorrow we will start you in a school."

We were all curious as to what kind of school, so one guy got the courage to ask, "What type of school?" It happened to be a mobile laundry school, and we were supposed to maintain the units. We shaped up our act and marched through downtown, and even the cars waited for us at the stop lights. They marched us to the Wolford Hotel. We found out there were 300 soldiers going to this special school in a town of 30,000. There were fifty soldiers in each hotel and six hotels in the downtown area. The course took three months to complete.

They made me a temporary squad leader. It was authority with no extra pay, but it did have its advantages. We had to make a bed check at 11 P.M., and of course, we were supposed to be in bed, too. There were plenty of girls around, so I started going with a cute little chick named Mary Lou. She was like Muriel, she wanted to neck but that was all. So I told her if I wanted to neck I would go out with her, but if I wanted something else, I would go out with someone else. After a couple of weeks of that, she decided she didn't want to share me anymore and gave in. She was a virgin, and the first few times I had a hell of a time getting it in. I guess part of the trouble was the position we had to do it in, either standing against a fence or standing in the alley.

The other squad leader's name was Jerry. His room was down the hall from us on the seventh floor. Jerry would swap with my roommate and sleep up there with me so we could sneak Mary Lou and her girlfriend into the room. Jerry's girlfriend was a "nice" girl, too (no hanky-panky). One night Mary Lou and I were in bed and in the saddle, and we could hear Jerry and Louise arguing. Jerry would say, "They are doing it," and Louise would say, "No they're not!" Finally Jerry said, "I will show you Louise," and turned on the light. Louise let out a scream but Jerry still did not get any. After that, Louise would come up with Mary Lou and wait for us to enjoy ourselves since they were supposed to be out together. On Saturdays in Danville, we had go to the park to do exercises and close-order drills. Sometimes we took hikes with light field packs because we did not have our rifles. An eighteen- or twenty- mile hike was the average on Saturdays. I don't know why, but they picked me to set the pace. I would ask them what time they wanted to get back to town, and most said as soon as possible. I set the pace, and with a little double time, we would get back into town about 1:30 in the afternoon. We would then have the rest of the day off as well as all day Sunday. We always had a bed check unless there were some guys who lived close enough to get an overnight pass.

Most of the guys had girlfriends, and the people in town were really nice. I got acquainted with a guy named Ed and his wife. He was the head of the water department. I can't remember her name. They were really nice people and would invite me and a buddy over for Sunday night dinner, good fried chicken or whatever, and in their garden were some of the best tomatoes I've ever eaten, as well as all the other stuff that comes out of a garden in late July and early August. When it was tomato-picking time, they never had have enough help to harvest the crop, so instead of taking hikes or some kind of drills, we would pick their tomatoes. We enjoyed that because it gave us extra money. Also while in Danville, we pulled our own M.P. duty. Being a temporary squad leader, I would be in charge, giving me no restrictions on curfew, so I pulled this duty about once a week. After the bed check at 11 P.M., the squad leader and I would go downtown in some of the bars. They gave us free drinks in the back room if we wanted them. There weren't many guys missing bed check because they didn't want to get into trouble. If they did, they could end up getting kicked out of school and leaving the good town of Danville.

Once in a while the air force guys would come over from Chanute Field, especially on the weekends. They would be surprised to see M.P.s on duty. We would make them toe the mark, because we didn't want competition with the girls. Danville would also let us use the bowling alleys for free when no one was using them, we had to set our own pins. I would generally set the first game, then the loser would have to set the next. Since I bowled a few times in Elcho, Wisconsin, which used to cost twenty-five cents a game, I had a little more experience than some, so usually I wouldn't have to rack anymore pins that day!

After completing our school training in Danville, I had to tell Mary Lou good-bye. To our surprise, we went back to Cheyenne for more advanced training. The first thing I did was call up Muriel. Although we had written to each other infrequently, we started to date again, going roller skating and to the movies, riding bicycles for two, etc. But as usual, I would have to see some other girlfriends for more than smooching. I respected Muriel for that, but it was upsetting me that couldn't get past first base. She did introduce me to her folks, who were fine people. Sometimes they invited my buddy and me to have Sunday dinner with them. Muriel's dad and I hit it off because he loved to play checkers, which I had learned to play on cold Wisconsin nights from lumberjacks and farmers. Anyway, it was very seldom I could beat Muriel's dad at checkers. Muriel's dad did not smoke, so I started smoking cigars, and when we started playing checkers, I would light up a cigar and nonchalantly blow smoke in his face. That way I would win a few games.

One night Bob, Vera, Muriel, and I went to a show. As we were walking back home (at least now I could walk her home after meeting her folks), we walked through a park. Bob and Vera decided to go to the other side of the park, but Muriel and I stayed where we were. We were laying on a side hill, necking, pretty heavily when Muriel said, "Wait a minute, I don't want to ruin my nylons." I thought to myself, Well I'm going to get it tonight. Was I ever wrong! But since there are many willing girls, I didn't have to force myself on her, even though I was a little pissed off that Bob made out. So I didn't call Muriel for a couple of weeks.

One day at camp, I got sick, running a fever. I wound up in the hospital on base. When they took me into the infirmary, I didn't have a toothbrush, shaving stuff or anything. I called Muriel up to see if she would bring me the things I needed, and she agreed. When she came in with the captain, I thought to myself, Boy did I lose out. She also told me came out on his motorcycle. I must have looked shocked, because she told me he was her cousin who had stopped by to see the family. After that we started to go together again.

While on our second tour of Fort Warren, our company, 200 men, went on bivouac at Pole Mountain. We had to walk twenty-eight miles with a full field pack. My squad was on flank guard. We were out in the woods, checking for any enemy behind every rock. Art T. and I were coming up on a draw when we saw a jeep. We crawled up over a little ledge curious to see what they were doing. We waited for a little while, and then they set off a smoke flare, which was supposed to be mustard gas. We put on our gas mask, sneaked up behind them, and poked our rifles in their backs. Of course, our rifles were not loaded, but it scared the hell out of them. One was a colonel and one was a major. We told them they were the enemy, so we could not give them a break. I said to Art T., "Get the jeep." So, the two officers walked in front of the jeep and I sat on the hood with my rifle trained on them. They had to walk back about one and a half miles to get to our main company, and they were pissed. Our commanding officer said we should not have been so hard on them, but we asked how he would treat an enemy. He gave in, and so did the colonel and the major. They said we had done a good job.

In the meantime, I went out for boxing. While the rest of the troops were out in the field exercising and marching, I was in the gym working out. While in Fort Warren, I only had three bouts, all of which I won.

We were all tired of basic training and not going overseas, so five of us decided to join the paratroopers. We got permission for a physical which we all passed. We went to our commanding officer to sign the papers for the transfer, but our commanding officer said he could not transfer us because the company would be understaffed, especially since we would be shipping out in two weeks. (Shipping-out time was supposed to be confidential.) I had a few more dates with Muriel, but the last night before we shipped out, I could not get off the base, so she came out to see me by bus. We walked down by the creek where the guards would not see us, and there was a lot of hugging and kissing. Of course, I wanted something else, but she said "What if I got pregnant and you would be gone or killed?" So I agreed with her, and we bid our farewell. She caught the last bus back to town.

The next morning we boarded a train. When the train stopped, we were in Columbus, Ohio. Of course, on the train there wasn't any goofing off like when we went to Danville. We didn't go to Fort Hayes, which was an induction center. Instead, we went to the army depot, which was a warehouse for military supplies. We worked right with civilians, which we all liked since there were lots of women there. The bigshot that ran the depot had the women pretty scared of us, but it took only a week or two to break the ice. There was one I took a shine to; her nickname was Mousey. We would go down some aisles, behind some boxes, and swap some kisses.

Not being from Fort Hayes but being in the service for nine months, we learned how to look sharp for a G.I. Also, we could wear garrison caps which were dressier than the so-called piss caps. We would go to downtown Columbus, get off the bus at Broad and High Streets, hit a few night spots, drink some boilermakers (an order of a beer and glass of whiskey), drop the glass of whiskey in the beer, and drink it down. Some of the girls would do the same. I soon found out that was not the smartest thing to do. Drinking boilermakers may have been macho, but it would goof a guy up so they couldn't enjoy the gals. There were plenty of girls there that worked at the defense plant, and they all had plenty of money. The first week after payday, our money situation was always good, but after that it would go downhill. We would have to be in at 10 P.M. for bed check, but on weekends we could get a weekend pass, and not have to be back for bed check until Sunday night. What a few of us would do when we were broke would be to borrow twenty-five cents from somebody and get on a bus for Broad and High. We would stand there on the sidewalk until a car would drive up with some gals in it who would ask, "What are you doing tonight soldier?" If you didn't like their looks, you could say you were waiting for a date. If you liked their looks, you would get in. One night a couple of good-looking gals drove up, and I accepted their invitation. We were looking for a buddy of mine to go with us, so we were hitting the bars where I knew they hung out but no one seemed to like their looks. That night I wound up with the two of them. I had to stay in camp a week after that because I got a strain!

There were three of us that found this little bar called "Old Corners," in an Irish settlement. The first night there, I picked up this gal. We had a few dances, and she said she was getting hot. We didn't know where to go, so we went and found a dark sidewalk. I laid down overcoat, and we had our fun. Then she said, "If you can do it again, I'll give you twenty dollars." Since twenty dollars would give me some poker money for camp. After that, whenever I was low on money, I would call her up and meet her at the Old Corner bar.

One night I met another gal who had a car, a 1930 Chevrolet. The next day was Sunday, and my money was almost gone. I asked her if she would take me to the depot or loan me a quarter. She said "Why don't you take the car and come back next weekend?" After "twisting my arm" to take the car, I agreed! I was still smooching Mousey at work, so I asked her if she wanted to go to a dance. I knew she didn't have a car, so I told her I had borrowed one. It was only the middle of the week, but I took Mousey out. We didn't have much time to dance because I had to be back to the depot at 10 P.M. and she had brought a girlfriend along. Of course, while her girlfriend was dancing, we made use of the car. Columbus was certainly a fun time while I was there.

We took all of our winter clothes when we shipped out the first part of February 1944. Again, we were guessing where we were going. Of course, most of us thought E. T. O. because of our clothes. We were wrong and ended up at Camp Stoneman, California.

Our company was doing a lot of hiking to keep in shape. One day as we were hiking, it was raining lightly. We came to this hill which was fairly steep and muddy off the side of the road. The company commander said the first twenty that made it over the hill would get a weekend pass. Well, the guys that went first were trying to stand up and climb the hill. Jack B. and I were in rough march together, and I asked Jack if he wanted a weekend pass. Of course, he said yes. I said, "Sling your rifle and follow me. We can clean up when we get back to camp." We climbed on all fours and were among the first ten over the top, earning the weekend pass.

We got our pass, got into a military bus, and got off at downtown Oakland. The first thing we did was hail a cab. We asked him to take us to where we could find some girls. Well, he took us to a place called Pinocchio. There were a bunch of good-looking gals dancing together and sitting around. Jack and I looked at each other and thought, boy, this is the place. We went up to the bar and ordered a beer. The bartender gave us a beer, and as we were looking around to see which one we were going to ask to dance, the bartender said, "Boys, I don't think you belong in here." We asked why. He said, "You are looking for girls, aren't you?"

We said "Yup!"

He said, "Those aren't girls, they are men acting like women, and they each have their own lover." We couldn't get out of there fast enough. We finally decided the cab driver didn't like G.I.s. So we took in the sights that weekend without gals.

After two weeks in Camp Stoneman, we boarded a liberty ship. There were 4,500 G.I.s on board, and we headed across "the puddle" without an escort. The food they served was unbelievable. I believe the captain made a bunch of money on meals alone. They only served two meals a day. In the morning we had hard-boiled eggs, moldy bread, and oatmeal with powdered milk. In the afternoon we had wieners, moldy bread, and sauerkraut.

The ship was manned by merchant marines. They were eating three meals a day and having the best steak, pork chops, etc. What they had left over, they would pass through a porthole from their mess hall to us.

Well, the guys would scramble and fight for the food. I said to one of our buddies that I would have to be damn hungry before I would get in there and fight for that food. Every day we would sit on the open deck and smell the aroma of their food cooking. After about three weeks, I couldn't sit by anymore, and I dove in. I came out with a half-eaten pork chop. Boy, did that taste good. I think I chewed on the bone for two hours, just like a puppy.

We would play penny-ante poker on the ship. When I ran out of money, I would strap on my rifle belt and head over to the officers quarters. Since most of the time we were in swim trunks, the M.P.s couldn't tell if we were officers or enlisted men. With my rifle belt on, I could, therefore, pass as an officer. The officers quarters had cold water through a refrigerated water dispenser, while all we had to drink was our water out of canvas bags which was hot and tasted like hell. Since some of the guys pay fifty cents for a canteen of ice-cold water, I figured I could make some money. I would walk up to the M.P. guarding the officers quarters door, and give him a sharp salute. He would salute back, and I would walk in and fill the canteen with water. Then I would walk around the hallways awhile so I wouldn't have to come right back out. I'd leave, saluting the M.P. again. It helped to keep me in poker money.

We waved at the Hawaiian Islands as we went by. We had three submarine attacks on the way. The captain of the ship would change course every forty-five seconds, because it takes a sub a minute or more to zero in. And then they would roll out and shoot off depth charges from the aft of the ship. I saw one of the periscopes. Also while we were under a sub attack, I was at the bow of the ship. As the ship was changing course, I was leaning to one side; I looked straight down and there went a torpedo missing the ship by about twelve feet. It really put a scare into me.

After a couple of weeks out, they wanted volunteers for exhibition boxing. Being bored, I volunteered. While I was in the ring fighting one guy— and doing quite well—someone slid their life jacket into the ring. While I was moving and dancing around, I stepped back onto the edge of the jacket. My knee popped out of its joint. It popped right back in, but I went down. So they took me to sickbay and put an elastic bandage on it. They gave me a relaxer and told me to lay there for a while.

Fighting in the ring, all I had on were my G.I. boxer shorts, so that was all I had on while lying on the table in sickbay. I fell asleep and dreamed.

I was with Fritz E., a friend in the Navy, and his girlfriend, a high-class woman. We were at a dance, sitting there drinking beer at a table. Some nice dance music came on, and Fritz asked his girlfriend to dance. They were getting along fine dancing, but when the dance was over, Fritz reached down between her legs from behind, pulled her feet out from under her, made her fall forward. As she fell forward, he caught her and carried her back to the table. I was laughing and said to Fritz, "Boy, that is a new way to carry them off the floor." Well she was really put out about the whole thing. I started talking to her, telling her not to be mad at Fritz because he was only kidding. But she kept on saying that she never wanted to see him again. So Fritz walked off to another table. This gal said to me that she didn't want to stay there anymore and asked if I could drive. I said sure.

So she said "Let's go for a ride while I settle down." She had a 1941 Lincoln Club Coupe. We were driving down this wide gravel road with deep ditches, about eight feet deep, and a nice slope. She said, "Stop," so I stopped and we got out. She led me down into the ditch. She laid down and closed her eyes, just laying there. I was sitting down a little past her feet. All at once, she pulled up her legs and bent her knees. I saw she didn't have any panties on. I sat there for a bit and said to myself, This is an opportunity I am not going to miss. So I jumped in the saddle and put it in. She really came to life and liked it.

Well, it made me mad because she had gotten so mad at Fritz, and I yelled, "You women are all alike, you want to f—- but you don't want to admit it."

At about the same time, I sat up on the table trying to figure out where I was. There were about five sailor medics laughing their butts off at me. I was embarrassed, but by then it was too late.

The first stop was Oro Bay in New Guinea, where some of the troops debarked. I have no idea how many. We were there two days and nights. Then we moved on and went to Lae, New Guinea. It took us thirty days to get there from San Francisco. We were off-loaded and sent to a location where we were supposed to set up a temporary camp. Lae was supposed to be secure from the Japanese. Our camp was alongside a peaceful, flowing stream. The moon shone bright. It was like a movie setting of the south sea islands with the mountains in the background. At this camp we had two-man tents because we would be here very long. We were called a bastard outfit because we only had 200 men. Since we were a small group, they let us set up our tents at random. Well, you could see where the river banks were, and they were a little way from the river. But some of the guys thought it would be nice to be close to the river so they wouldn't have far to go in the morning to wash up. I mentioned to our squad leader, Mucha, that I didn't think it would be to wise to put our tents down by the river bottom. I had to explain to him that if it starts to rain up in the mountains, that water was going to go right down there. Well, old Mucha wasn't too much of a squad leader, but he did listen to that so our squad set up our tents on the banks above the cut in the river. We had cots and mosquito nets, and because it was so warm, most of the tent sides were rolled up. It was after midnight before everything really settled down. Unfortunately, about half of the company set up down by the river, including our sergeant, and first sergeant, who wanted to be close to the river so they could wash up in a hurry. I don't know if the bugler was down by the river or not, but when he blew reveille, the guys down by the river, sat up and put their hands over the side of their cot. Their shoes, clothes, and whatever else they had laying on their duffle bag, as well as the bag, were was heading for the ocean. It had rained up in the mountains and the river had gone up. One sergeant I talked to said that early in the morning before reveille, he accidentally put his hand over the side of the cot and felt water. He said he thought he was dreaming. But when he went to sit up, he knew he wasn't. It was pretty funny watching the guys running around borrowing clothes and shoes, trying to find ones that would fit. They all moved to higher ground that day.

For about a week we didn't do anything because the company didn't have an assignment. All we did was hunt for souvenirs and swim. There was a well with a box that was partly broken open. We never thought of hooking onto it and bringing it up. Finally, a buddy did, and inside was a Japanese dagger with a jade handle. It was beautiful. He certainly was lucky.

We didn't have a mess hall, so we had to eat outside. Only the cooks had a shelter. One day it was really raining and we all had our ponchos on. We were standing in the chow line when someone yelled, "Jap!." We found were two Japanese in the chow line wanting something to eat. One threw up his arms while the other took off running. We got our rifles and went looking for him in the tall grass. A friend of mine came upon him. He tried to take David's rifle away, and David had to shoot him. A few more came down off the mountains, but they just gave up without a fight.

We moved further inland and set up a more permanent camp. Now we had five-men tents. There was no floor to these tents. After about a month of scrounging around, we found where we could get some 2 by 12 lumber. At the time, I was driving a 6 by 6, but all I was supposed to do was haul troops to a gasoline pumping station where our company worked pumping aviation fuel off tankers and into fifty-five gallon drums, then stacking them five high on their sides. We talked Mucha into talking to Lieutenant Morrey. He asked what the plans were. We explained that if we had a 6-by-6 and an order to pick up only so many planks for the gasoline dump, we could get enough to put floors in our tents by diverting some of the load. Lieutenant Morrey thought it was a good idea, so our squad, including Lieutenant Morrey, went down to the docks and got a truck load. It took about four loads to do the whole company, and we had to do some conning to get more than we ordered. After that, it was up to our squad to go get rations, etc. Even our commanding officer thought our squad was nothing but a bunch of con artists. When we went after food rations, we were supposed to get so many cases of this and that, but when we were throwing them on the truck, we would start arguing how many were already loaded. One would say less, the other more, and all the time the rest of us would keep on throwing. The sergeant or corporal checking the list would get confused because someone would be talking to him most of the time. The mess sergeant couldn't believe all the rations we got that way. The only thing we couldn't get was meat. All the rations we were getting were canned or dehydrated, like milk, eggs, potatoes, etc., and when that ran out, we were back on "C" rations. Once a month we would get some kind of canned meat. One month it would be Spam the next some other kind of meat. One month we got a supply of Australian mutton. It stank so bad we could hardly get near the mess hall.

The cooks tried to camouflage the taste, and that was when I decided to eat hot peppers. The peppers grew wild over there, so I planted two plants outside our tent. When I went to chow, I would pick a couple of peppers. Some of the other guys did the same.

One day just after leaving the gasoline dump, the Japanese blew it up. We were only half a mile away. We stopped and watched the fireworks for about twenty minutes. Drums of gas would fly up 100 to 200 feet before exploding.

Just prior to the dump being blown up, our squad was stacking drums and it was raining harder than hell. Everyone else but our squad was standing under a shelter where the gas was pumped into barrels. We thought, Why should we be out here while the rest stay out of the rain? So we went to get out of the rain, too, but our platoon sergeant yelled, "You guys get out there and stack barrels."

I said "Damn it, sarge, we don't like the idea that everyone else is under a cover and we have to work." That evening Mucha came over and said the sergeant wanted to see me in his tent. Mucha went along. I went in his tent and he had a chair waiting for me. The sarge told me to sit down, so I did. He then said that he was going to court-martial me. I asked why, and he said for insubordination. I said, "I did not call you any name, and we did go back to work."

He then said, "What I should do is take you out in the jungle and beat the shit out of you."

I stood up and said, "What are you waiting for?" The sarge again told me to sit down. The sarge then said that he thought the men were getting away with too much and that he had to set an example. He decided it would be me. So he gave me a thirty-day restriction to the company area. I said to the guys, "If you can get some sugar, yeast, raisins, or any kind of canned fruit, I will make some jungle juice." They were happy about that because only once in a while would they get a couple of cans of beer. Our tent was close to the mess hall, and when they came back with the rations, they backed the truck in so that the officers couldn't see them unloading. They got the ingredients: 700 pounds of sugar, a case of raisins, a case of canned blackberries and dried apricots, and 50 pounds of yeast. I told them that we didn't need much yeast, but they said that was all they could find. Now where hide all that stuff? We made shelves above our cots with the lumber. We put the sugar up there because it would stay dryer up there than under the floor. We then cut a hole in the floor two planks wide and about three feet long, dug out the dirt, put three water cans down there plus the yeast, because the can was too hard to hide elsewhere. I didn't have much knowledge about how to make wine, but what I knew was a lot more than the rest of them. The first batch we made was one five-gallon drum of raisin and one five-gallon can of blackberry. I told the guys that we would have to wait about thirty days, but after only three weeks, the guys were after me to try it. We tried the raisin first. It was a little yeasty but good. And it had a kick to it. Shortly after that, we had a day off. Since I was off my restriction by then, we decided to have a few drinks and play cards. We were getting pretty happy. There were five of us. We had a little Mexican fellow named Reese, and he was getting pretty loaded. We all decided that we should have our squad leader in on the party, so we sent Reese down to see him. When Reese got back, he said Mucha would be right up. Reese had two more drinks and passed out. When Mucha walked into our tent, he didn't know what to say. He just stood there.

Finally one of us said "Here, have a drink." He asked what it was, and we told him it was jungle juice. He asked us where we had gotten it, and we told him we had just gotten it, and if he wanted some that was fine, since we didn't think it was right to celebrate without our leader. That built up his ego. But we were all a little mad at him for not standing up to the sergeant on my court-martial deal. After a few drinks, we decided to go swimming. If we cut across the airstrip it was only a couple of miles. So Sherman, George, Ernie, Mucha, and I started out. We filled our canteens with jungle juice and headed out. We staggered across the airstrip and to the other side of the field. Near some aircraft gasoline belly tanks, Sherman passed out. George wasn't feeling any pain, but he decided to stay with Sherman. Now there was Ernie, Mucha, and me, and we made it to the beach. At the beach we stripped down to our shorts. There was coral there, but when you got out beyond waist deep, the coral ended and it was nice and sandy. Ernie and I walked carefully across the coral to where it was nice and sandy, but Mucha was pretty drunk by then and could hardly walk. We were calling, "Come on, Mucha, you can make it." Mucha was about six-feet-six-inches tall and lanky, and since he couldn't stand up very well, he tried to come out on his hands and knees. About the time he reached the end of the coral, a wave would come in and wash him back up on shore.

We were coaxing him on and on, and he kept on saying, "Really, boys, you think I am chicken shit, but really I am not." That was about all he could say. After half an hour of that, we thought we had better give up, so we went back to shore. Mucha just kept repeating that he wasn't chicken shit. His body was really scratched and bruised by the coral. Now he was so drunk he couldn't walk, so Ernie stayed with him. I went to a company close by and found a motor pool sergeant. I explained the situation and told him I would give him a canteen of jungle juice if he would take us to our company. When we got to the company, the sergeant drove the jeep down to Mucha's tent. We put him on his cot, and since no one else was in the tent, we didn't have to do any explaining. The next morning Mucha came up and asked who beat the shit out of him. Of course, Ernie asked him if he didn't remember swimming and trying to get past the coral. He said, "All I remember is walking across the airfield heading for the ocean." Mucha never did tell the sergeant what happened or where and how he got so drunk and bruised up. So we had a little more faith in him after that.

We also got a new lieutenant who had transferred in from a transportation company. He took a liking to me, Ernie, and George. While I was restricted to the company area, he would come down and play cards with us. When we started our wine business, he would come down to have some of whatever we had. Sometimes we would run out because the other half of our squad from the other tent would come over, and, if we weren't there, they would help themselves.

One evening, not too long after chow, First Lieutenant Bernie yelled out, "Diemel, front and center." What did I do now? I said to myself. The lieutenant said to get a couple of my buddies and we would all go for a ride, so we piled in the jeep. He drove us up to the officer's club, which was up on a hill with a nice view of the bay and terrain.

We said "We can't go in there."

But he said, "I know, but I can, and I thought you guys would like some stateside whiskey." The lieutenant went in and came out with a fifth. We just sat sipping on the bottle and watching the other officers in there dancing with the nurses and WAC's, everyone having a ball.

I asked Lieutenant Bernie, "How come you are sitting out here with us when you could be in there having a good time?"

He said, "I could, but there aren't any men in there, and I like to drink with men." That sure made us feel good. So after that, about once every two weeks, we would go up to the officer's club. We even took Mucha once, and Mucha was really surprised at what the lieutenant and we were doing. He was informed to keep his mouth shut.

Another time when we weren't working, Lieutenant Bernie again yelled, "Diemel, front and center." He asked me if I could drive a duck. I said sure. Then he said, "Let's go swimming with some Australian nurses."

I replied, "Hell, yes, let's go." We went over to his old transportation company and asked for a duck. When they asked who the driver would be, and he said Sergeant Diemel. They asked where my stripes were, and the lieutenant said that I don't wear them. I was just a ordinary buck private at the time. I didn't know it, but about three miles from where we were along the shore was an Australian convalescence hospital. The reason there wasn't a road was because of the Nayhab River. With the rains, they couldn't even keep a pontoon bridge because it would wash out. So, we dropped in the ocean with the duck and took off to the Aussies. When we got there, it had a beautiful beach—all sand—and the waves were just little swells. Before I beached the duck, Lieutenant Bernie saw this good-looking nurse with this heavyset, balding Aussie officer. He had freckles all over his baldness. Lieutenant Bernie told me beach it, and he jumped overboard and told the Aussie officer that he was taking over. When I got to shore, the nurses came around because they liked the Americans. I went swimming with three nurses. We did some underwater kissing because the other Aussie officers weren't too happy having us there. I made a date for another day, and so did Lieutenant Bernie, but we never went back.

While we were in Lae, New Guinea, there was a Japanese hospital that was built underground in a mountain. When we arrived there, all the entrances were blown shut (so they said). On top of this mountain there was an Aussie lookout and a radio relay station. They had strong telescopes to watch the ship activity. Well, David H. and I got to be great friends with them. We discovered their lookout while hunting for souvenirs. There were two Aussie officers ahead of us. On the trail that led up to their lookout, we saw a dead Jap. The Aussies saw a P-38 pistol on this Jap and made a grab for it, but the Jap was booby trapped and blew them up, killing one and wounding the other. We went up and told their Aussie buddies, who radioed down to their company to pick them up. The other trail we had taken before was steeper, but this one was easier for walking. We were told that if we looked for souvenirs and found a body, be sure to tie a strong string through a belt loop then get twenty to thirty feet away. Once behind something, we could pull the string and roll them over. I never found one booby trapped. When David H. and I weren't working or when we were working nights, we would go up on the hill because it was cool up there with a nice view. We would take our machetes and canteens with water and jungle juice. We would hack our way up the hillside through the underbrush. Once we came upon a trail that was covered by underbrush, and when we followed it for a little way, we found an entrance to the underground hospital. In fact, there were two entrances. It was horseshoe-shaped, in and out at the ends and in the center was the main entrance to the hospital. It was shaped like this:

We could see into the main entrance by the outside light, seeing the supporting timbers as well as some water. We made it up to the Aussie lookout after some rough climbing and told them what we had found. They were quite surprised, so after some conversation, we decided to go and look for some medical souvenirs. We would have to have a good flashlight and a rifle, as well as a long rope to tie onto us so that in case we got blown up by a mine or caught in a booby trap, they could pull us out. A week later we took the easy trail up to the Aussies and then back down the steep hillside to the shorter trail. We had no trouble finding the entrances. We estimated that the entrances were about twelve feet wide and eight feet high. Well, David H. and one of the Aussies tied a rope around us at the main entrance. When I said "us," it was the other Aussie, Jerry, and I. Jerry had his rifle, and I had a five-cell flashlight. When we first walked in, there wasn't any water, but as we got further in, we found water, so we walked slowly and cautiously. The water was getting deeper. I shone the light up on a timber, and I saw this large snakeskin. It was dead silence in there, spookier than all hell. A frog would croak, and we would just about grab each other, but we kept on going. First, the water was knee-deep, then waist-deep and finally we could see entrances to other rooms. We hoped we would find something. I was shining the light all around at the room entrances and timbers. Then I brought it down to the water in front of us, and I saw a ripple on the water. At the head of the ripple was a snake mouth heading right for us. I was so damned scared I couldn't yell, so in a low, scratchy voice I said to Jerry, "Get him!" Jerry shot, and the snake disappeared. So did we. We came out of there faster than we went in. We decided that wasn't for us and those souvenirs could stay there. I have been in some spooky places, but I don't think any will compare to that. But that didn't end our scrounging. One day we found some Japanese tunnels and decided to look around again. They were on the low side of the hills and easy to get at. We had our string and some rope. David was scared to go into the tunnel, so I said I would. I took a flashlight, and the first thing I saw was a dead Jap. There wasn't much left of the body, mostly bones and clothes. Nevertheless, I had to make sure there were no booby traps. I tied on the string, got out of the way, and pulled. Nothing happened. I did that twice more and then I found a larger opening where I found a box of Japanese .25 carbines that had never been opened. I also found some canned fish. The little round tins were smaller than our tuna cans nowadays. We dragged out the rifles and some of the caviar. We took one little taste of the caviar and threw the rest away. The rifles were still in cosmoline. I wanted to ship some home, but postal wouldn't allow it. I told the Aussie buddies about it, and they said they knew an Aussie major who would be interested. They could ship them home. So they gave me his name and where to find him. I went to see him when I had a chance. He was quite an outstanding person, with a good sense of humor. The deal we made was that he would give me one Phillip quart T of rum for one rifle. To me, that wasn't a very good deal, but then, any deal was better than none, and it was getting close to the time that we could be shipping out. I can't remember for sure, but I think there were thirty rifles. I would take one or two over at a time. It was about a three-mile walk each way. After a few conversations, he found out that I knew how to play cribbage. (In fact, I was nine years old when I first learned. Gus T. lived in Summit Lake, Wisconsin, and on cold winter nights, I would go down the little hill and see Gus. To pass the time, he taught me to play cribbage. We got to where we would play for a penny a point, and then if I lost all my money, he would give it back and we would start over.)

The Aussie major was fairly old, maybe in his fifties, and he kind of reminded me of Gus. So we would play cards and have a few drinks (rum), and once in a while he would give me an extra quart. We also got to be good friends. Just our tent knew about the rum, and we would get Coca-Cola syrup. With chlorine water, syrup, and rum, we would stay happy.

We also had flying foxes, the oversized bats with a wing spread of four or more feet. We had what we called the flying fox theater where on a moonlit night when it wasn't raining, you could see them circling above, forty or more of them. Sometimes at night, we would try to kill them. We would cut long bamboo poles, then shine a flashlight up in the air. They would dive at the light, and we would swing the bamboo poles back and forth. They sure were mean-looking S.O.B.s with their sharp teeth fox-like faces. Right outside of our tent grew a persimmon tree, and these flying foxes liked them. They would land on our tent and bounce around, feeding on a persimmon. One night there was a tut-tut-tut noise on our roof keeping us awake, so I decided to kill the flying fox making the noise. I came out from under the eave of the tent where I figured it would be. I had the broom back for a swing. I jumped out and turned on the light. That damned thing dove at the light, and I dove right back in the tent, face first on the floor. Of course, the guys all laughed and asked me what happened. I stayed in the tent after that.

We used to do some swimming at Lae because it had nice breakers coming in. We would swim like crazy to get behind a breaker, and then swim from behind to get up on top of the wave and ride it back into shore. While swimming one day I lost a gold-plated ID bracelet Muriel had sent me. The undertow was so great that all you had to do was dive from shore and glide with your hands out in front. The water was so clear and you could see a long way, but the slope was steep, and the undertow took you down fast. When the pressure became too great, we would fight like heck to get out of the undertow. Finally, with our air running out, we could see the sun shining above. Then all at once, we would pop to the surface. Believe it or not, after about a dozen trips, I found the bracelet. There were three of us diving for it. While swimming one time, I dislocated my shoulder because a big wave broke over me before I could get on top of it. It washed me to shore, and they had to take me to the hospital where I was laid up for a week. I had to be careful about swimming after that.

In the middle of September 1944, I ran a high fever, so they sent me to the hospital. They found out I had a bad case of tonsillitis. My tonsils were so inflamed that they had to get them down before they could operate. While I was in the hospital, word came down that our outfit was pulling out. The doctors said I couldn't go because I would be a hindrance to the company. I found out later that our outfit went to the Admiralties Islands. Because Lae was being phased out, they flew the twenty of us left behind down to Oro Bay and put us in a casualty camp. The camp was right next to an officer's club. There the officers were with nurses and WACs having a good time. They were drinking and swimming with the girls while all we could do was watch. They even had a high fence and M.P.s at the gates. The fence went out into the ocean a fair distance with M.P.s in a hut on stilts to watch that no enlisted man would try to come in their area. The only clothes I had were on my back, and my shoes were a pair of cutoff jungle boots. I didn't even have a cap. So I budded up with a sailor who had an extra sailor's hat and an extra pair of swim trunks.

After being at Lae where all the white women stayed with the officers, I was ready for a date. So, one day I said to this sailor, named Ed, "Let's go to the officer's club and have a few drinks." Ed wondered how we were going to do that. I told him, "The officers are in their swim trunks, so the M.P.s won't know the difference. All we have to do is swim way out in the bay and come to shore in the middle of their area. When we are ready to leave, we just give the M.P.s a return salute and walk out the gate. While we are there, we just have to act like we know what we are doing." It worked like a charm. They even had cold beer. We talked and swam with nurses and WACs. We couldn't make a date, though, because we had no other clothes, and if they found out that we were E.M.s it would ruin our whole deal. Even so, we had quite a bit of fun just the way it was. We met some of the same girls for a swim and drinks as well. They never asked too many questions, and we never told them too much. But we did dance with them.

Right in front of the hospital grew a banana tree, and it had a stalk of bananas on it which were just about ripe. The hospital also had a nice lawn in front. Four or five of us really wanted those bananas, but we couldn't get them easily from the ground, and we didn't want to cut down the tree. That would take too long, and we didn't want to ruin it. So, before anyone else could get the bananas, I suggested we swipe a six by six truck, drive along-side, break off the stalk, and leave. We borrowed a 6 by 6, but when we drove across the lawn, we sunk in about eight to twelve inches. It was around mid-night. We took the bananas to our tent and parked the truck down the road. The next day deep ruts were across the lawn, and the bananas were gone. There were lots of questions asked because the hospital staff was really pissed, but no one knew anything.

When I got to the Admiralties, we landed on Los Negroes, but we only found that our company was gone from there. No one knew where they went. Then I caught a small ship to Finchhaven, New Guinea, and from there to Hollandia, New Guinea. That is when I found that my outfit had gone to Leyte Philippine Islands, with the first calvary. In Hollandia the first sergeant had a parrot, and every morning at daybreak, that parrot would strut down through the tent, whistle loudly, and say, "Get up, you son-a-bitches." He kept it up until all the casualties got up.

One day I was over there by a small airport and a sergeant was working on a Piper Cub. He was getting nervous because the lieutenant that had the plane wanted to take it up in a couple of hours, and he couldn't get it to run on the right mag or both mags. He was changing mags like mad. So I just took a screwdriver, put it in the cap, held onto the metal, and gave it a hand spin. I told the sarge that this mag was okay because I got a good shock. He asked me what I knew about planes. I said a little bit. The sergeant asked me to help him. It didn't take long to find that the trouble was in the switch. When the lieutenant came to take a ride, he asked the sergeant if found the trouble. The sergeant said, "Yes, sir, but I didn't find it, he did," pointing to me. That was one time my aviation schooling came in handy. The lieutenant asked me if I wanted to go for a ride with him. I said sure. We flew around a while. After we got back, he told me if I would be there tomorrow, we would go for another ride. Then he tried to talk me into transferring to his outfit to be his mechanic. His outfit was a medical. But I told him that I wanted to get back to my buddies.

It was hard getting up to Leyte because most of the ships that came into port didn't want to go into a combat area if they didn't have to. Fourteen guys, including me, caught a ride on a small tanker. The food was good, but we had to sleep on the open deck with a tarp stretched above us in case it rained and also to protect us from the sun. After ten days, they let us off at Biak, a small island. We went back to dehydrated food and "C" rations.

It was Christmas Eve and we heard there was a ship in from stateside, so this friend and I talked it over and decided to go check it out. Maybe we could get some fresh fruit, beer, or anything. When we got to the ship and started up the gangplank, we were stopped by their shore patrol. We told him we would like to see their mess sergeant or whatever the navy called him. We could hear music and singing, so we knew they were celebrating. We found out that they couldn't leave the ship, but they did allow us on board, and we found the guy in charge of the galley. They didn't have any fruit, but they did have cold-storage eggs and fresh potatoes. We traded some dutch money for three dozen eggs and half an orange crate of potatoes. He also gave us four beers.

It was a three-mile walk back to our camp. We carried the crate together sometimes or alone. When we got back to camp, it was around 11 P.M., so we went into the kitchen and borrowed (yes, borrowed) a can of Australian butter, salt and pepper, and a camping-type Coleman stove with just one little burner. It was midnight when we started cooking. With those potatoes cooking in butter in our mess gear, the aroma was drifting through the camp. The other guys woke up, got their mess gear, and started standing in line outside of our tent. We told them they would have to get their own, because that's what we had to do. It was one of the best Christmas Eve meals I have ever had. At least, that's the way I remember it. We had to guard the rest of our potatoes and eggs after that night because everyone wanted some. It was only a few days before they were all gone.

Finally a ship came by and said they would take the bunch of us to Leyte even though they knew it was a combat area. It was a Hawaiian ship named Maui. I was still wearing the sailor's cap given to me earlier, and when we boarded the ship, the officer in charge said, "You eight sailors over there. You will be the auxiliary gun crew on the 95 mm at the aft." I started to say I wasn't navy. Then my buddy explained to me that we get to sleep on the open deck and not in the hot holds with the G.I. troops, so I kept my mouth shut. I did say, though, that I didn't know anything about a 95 mm, and he said that I didn't have to. If needed, all we would have to do would be to pass the ammunition. The only scare we had was when we were coming into

Leyte Gulf, and a couple of Japanese Betties flew around. But they had so much gunfire from other ships that it wasn't even close.

Our lone company of 200 men was in charge of six different dumps (storage places), so-called because that was where they "dumped" the supplies off. When the guys that were left came into the tent, they about fell over, because they thought I would never make it back. Most of these guys were in my squad. Our company had quite a few casualties. Lieutenant Bernie was still there; he got killed a little later in a typhoon. There was a little celebrating going on. I started driving truck right away, hauling Philippine civilians that were working at different dumps plus hauling whatever was in demand.

So I was back with the old company again. I found out they were still in the jungle juice business. At the C&E Dump, a clothing and equipment dump, they had a bomb shelter built out of tents. It was like an Eskimo igloo. These tents were folded up and stacked about twelve deep, which was pretty good in case of an air raid. That was where they hid the jungle juice. At the time, all they had was blackberry, which tasted pretty good. Sherman C. and George D. were the top makers, and since our company was in charge of the dumps, they could get whatever was available. Lieutenant Bernie was in on it. So whenever I was at the C&E Dump, they would have to take me into the shelter to sip a few. We also had three-man foxholes dug at our company area in case of an air raid. At night when Washmachine Charlie flew over, all dove into the foxholes. It would be a Japanese Zero or a Betty. We could usually tell a Zero by the sound. He would circle way up high just to keep us awake, and every once in a while he would drop a bomb or two. W.G., a good buddy of mine, got so tired of it that he said to hell with it every time the air raid alarm sounded. He just stayed in his tent and never got a scratch, while some of the others in the foxholes got blown away or wounded. We had lots of other raids besides Washmachine Charlies. They happened mostly in the daytime, but Charlie kept us awake at night. I told the guys about the P-51s that could out-maneuver a Zero, and they thought I was giving them B.S. It took two P-38s to get a Zero. The 38s were faster, but they couldn't maneuver as well, so one would fly higher while the other sat on his tail. Suddenly, the higher one would come from above to try to get him. We used to listen to the pilots talk on the radio at a communication place. That was the only reason I knew about it. But the first P-51s came in when we were on Leyte.

Our company area was on White Beach. That was where the landing was made on October 20, 1944, at 10:00 A.M.

Taclobon was about four miles away. That was the closest town of any size, and we had some men there taking care of a warehouse. I was driving a six by six hauling personnel during shift change as well as other items during regular working hours. A good buddy in our squad decided to make some extra money since we were able to haul civilians. So W.G. and a couple of other guys set up a small wall tent across a rice paddy behind our company. We hung up some G.I. blankets for partitions and found a couple of Filipino gals willing to make some extra money. So a couple of times a week, I would pick up the girls and bring them to the tent. To get across the rice paddy to the tent without wading through the paddy, we pulled some coconut logs into a line. W.G. was charging five or ten dollars for the girls. It didn't cost me anything because I was hauling them back and forth. Sherman C. was a virgin from Missouri and was really shy about girls. W.G. and I kept after him to try it. After a time he agreed, and W.G. said he could have it for free. So one evening Sherman and I walked over the logs. I took one girl on one side of blanket, and Sherman on the other. When I got through I asked Sherman how he was doing. He said, "I can't get a hard on."

I said, "Have her play with it," and I pulled the blanket down enough so I could motion to the gal to get a hold of it. (They couldn't understand English very well.) She tried, but it was no use. I was laughing because Sherman had been so excited about going, but he didn't say a word as we left. When we got back to our tent, I asked him what went wrong. He finally told me that when he had been trying to put the rubber on he came, which ruined it. About a week later, we took care of that, and he became a regular customer for W.G. One evening Jack B. was walking the logs back to camp after visiting the tent. He was pretty loaded on rice whiskey. Chuck C. was headed for the tent, and he wasn't feeling any pain either. There was no way for them to get past each other without one ending up the rice paddy, but neither one was going to turn around and go back, so they got into a argument. Both of them were big men, six feet tall and over two hundred pounds. I don't know who hit who first. I got it from some of the other fellows that all at once one was sitting straddled on the log. Then he pulled the other one down until both were straddling the log, feet and legs dangling in the rice paddy. Jack stared at Chuck and then took a big swing. He hit him alongside the head. Chuck swayed and was about to fall in the paddy, but then he got his bearings and wham, he hit Jack. The same would then happen to Jack. Sometimes it would take thirty seconds to a minute before one would swing. There were about thirty of us on the edge of the rice paddy watching the action. It was pretty funny. After this went on about five minutes, they both got off the log into the rice paddy to let each other pass. I don't know if Chuck got a gal that night or not, because those rice paddies were pretty stinky.

Another time, W.G. and I were walking back from Taclobon, and it was darker than hell. As we were walking by this engineer outfit, we saw a jeep in front of the officer's tent. W.G. said that he was tired of walking all the time and was going to swipe that jeep. I said, "Are you crazy? What about the guards?"

He said, "Hell, there aren't any guards." So I acted the lookout. There were a few lights on in some of the tents at that time because the blackout had been lifted.

This was about 10:30 or 11:00 P.M., and W.G. started into the company area when a guard hollered out, "Halt! Who's there?"

W.G. said, "Harry." The guard said, "Harry who?" Well W.G. couldn't think of a last name, so we took off running. We got back to camp, and I went to bed. I thought W.G. went to bed too.

It was a little after midnight when W.G. said, "Esky, wake up. I got it."

I said, "Got what?" I was still half asleep.

He said, "I got the jeep." That woke me up in a hurry but I thought he was B.S.ing. Sure enough, in the parking area was the jeep. He asked, "Where are we going to hide it?" I thought for a minute then I remembered a small grove of banana trees right by our company. In fact, it was right behind our commanding officer's tent. We drove it in there, threw some banana leaves over it, and left. The next night after work, we had to make sure it was still there. It was. So we went and told our motor pool sergeant about it, and we asked if he would paint a new number on it. He did, and after that we could park it in the parking area. But the sergeant made one mistake. He used the same number that was on one of our lieutentant's jeeps. Of course the lieutentant asked the motor pool sergeant whose jeep it was. He told him that W.G. and Esky had it. The lieutentant came to us and told us we would have to change our number because we couldn't have two jeeps with the same number, especially since his jeep was hot also. I went down to a salvage yard found a jeep I knew they would never be able to repair. I wrote the number off it. That really worked. We borrowed a bunch of trip tickets. Whenever we wanted to go somewhere, we would fill one out just in case the M.P.s would stop us to check. It was a Ford jeep, and it was faster than a Willy. Now W.G. could haul the girls back and forth in style, and we could go to Taclobon, to any of the night spots, or anywhere we wanted. That lasted a little over two weeks. One night W.G. and three other guys were going on a night out. They had some beer and rice whiskey. W.G. was telling them how fast the jeep was. They went to Tanawan and somehow got on the airstrip there to give the jeep a good tryout, because there were no paved roads on Leyte. Well, W.G. turned the jeep over. Two of the boys took off and left W.G. with the other guy. They were trying to upright the jeep when the M.P.s came. They asked "Whose jeep is that?" and both said, "We don't know." They asked who was driving, and again they said they didn't know. W.G. and the other guy convinced the M.P.s that they were hitchhiking to Tanawan when two guys picked them up. They had some beer and some rice whiskey. Then they all went to a dance and the guys in the jeep said that they would take them back to camp. The next thing they knew, they were on the airstrip with the jeep turned over. W.G. said that when he came to, the other guys were gone. He said they didn't know how they were going to get back to camp. The M.P.s bought the story and brought W.G. and his buddy back to camp. It was around 2:00 A.M. when W.G. woke me and told me the story and that we didn't have a jeep anymore. It was a good thing W.G. forgot to write a trip ticket, because the M.P.s confiscated the jeep. They never did find out to whom it belonged, because they were still driving it when we left White Beach.

While we were on White Beach, we swiped about fifteen chickens from the natives so we could have some fresh meat. We had a pen next to the rice paddy. We had the means to cook them in our tent with a little single-burner portable stove and our mess gear. Anyway, one evening the food at the mess hall wasn't very good, so we told Ruiz, a Mexican kid in our squad, to go out and wring a chicken's neck. We would get things ready in the tent, and then we would have a little chicken to split up. There were four of us splitting the chicken that night. Ruiz was from Los Angeles, but we figured he would know how to wring a chicken's neck if anyone did. He didn't come back, and we waited and waited and waited. Finally we thought we better go out and see what was taking so long. We went out and watched for a little while. He had the chicken by the legs and was swinging it around. He would stop, and the chicken would say "Awk, awk," really low. We went over and asked what he was doing. He said the chicken wouldn't die. We killed the chicken, but the bones in the poor thing were so mangled that we just threw it away. It was a while before we had fried chicken after that.

Sherman C., the virgin, also dispatched army ducks used to off-load ships out in the bay. The supplies were then sent to one dump or another. But one duckload of beer came in, and when Sherman C. said C&E Number 2, the driver questioned Sherman about the dispatch. Sherman told the driver that he had heard him right the first time. Sherman knew that most of our squad was working there with Lieutenant Bernie. The beer was a load of Schlitz in the brown, long-neck bottles, and Sherman knew that it wasn't a regular ration. When the duck pulled in to C&E Number 2, a clothing and equipment dump, Lieutenant Bernie told the men to get over and unload it and that they didn't need any civilians. I happened to be at the dump at the time. Boy, was it unloaded in a hurry and covered up. About a week later, a full bird colonel came around wondering what had happened to his beer. No one knew a thing about it, but we had some good beer for a while.

Sid L. was from Red River, Kentucky. He was quite a checker player, so not too many people played checkers with him, but we would get together to play. I could beat almost everyone else I played, but I couldn't beat Sid. Sid taught me quite a bit about checkers, and we would walk down to the Red Cross to play. We would play four or five different guys at the same time, just glancing at each board.

One Sunday, a navy lieutenant came into the Red Cross asking if anyone had a large refrigeration storage. He asked us, and Sid and I asked him why. He explained that on his ship a refer unit had gone out, and if they didn't get something done in a couple of days, they would have to dump the meat overboard. I asked what kind of meat. He said mostly beefsteak and roast with a little pork. I asked him what it would be worth to him, and he said he would split the meat fifty-fifty. I told him that we had a bunch of portable refer vans that he could probably use. He said good enough. So we found out where we could pick up the meat. They brought it to shore on an L.C.M. I told Sid to get a couple of guys and gas up a bunch of the refers to cool them. I went up to the motor pool to see if I could get a 6 by 6. When I explained to the motor pool sergeant what was going on, he was all for it. He even got a couple of extra guys to help, so we almost had two full 6 by 6 loads. By the time we had gotten everything worked out, it was more then eight hours later, but that just helped to get the vans cooled down. We filled up thirteen and a half vans, stacking it so it was easy to pick out what you wanted. Smitty was our mess sergeant, and by this time most of our squad was helping as well. I said to Smitty, "Smitty, keep these fourteen vans running, and when one gets empty you can shut it down." I also explained that the six and a half vans of meat were ours to use as we pleased.

Fresh, good meat was a great treat for us because mostly our fresh meat rations were very low. If we had fresh meat twice a week, that was great. Smitty was in high heaven cooking steaks, roasts, etc., and after about two weeks of this, the company commander asked Smitty, "Where are we getting all the steak and fresh meat from?"

Smitty said, "I don't know, all I know is what Diemel and W.G. told me and what was ours to use." The only reason Smitty included W.G. was because W.G. was with me when I told Smitty about the meat. We got called on the carpet, so we went into the C.O.s tent and gave him a salute. He asked where we got all the meat, and we explained the whole deal to him. He thought for a while and then said, "You know, you boys could be court-martialed for this."

I said, "No, sir."

Then he said, "Well, I will tell you one thing. You guys did one hell of a good job. Dismissed!"

We said, "Thank you sir," saluted, and left. It made us feel pretty good. A couple of weeks later at 11:00 at night, the chow whistle blew. It kept blowing. Everyone in camp got up to see what was wrong.

Here was Smitty saying, "Come on, boys, I am going to feed you. You guys are all a good bunch of sons-of-bitches." He had his cooks cooking up steaks like mad. We went inside and ate just to please Smitty. We figured all the bombing and strafing had gotten the best of him. It was the last we saw of Smitty. And Sergeant J., the one who gave me the summary court-martial down in New Guinea, was so scared that someone might bump Smitty off that he stayed in the officer's foxholes every time we had a raid.

One night we were in our tent talking when Bunji, a good Norwegian friend, got drunk. The discussion turned to New Guinea and Sergeant J., and Bunji grabbed his carbine and said, "I am going to kill that S.O.B." I had to run and tackle him or he might have. I sat out in the rain with him for about an hour talking like a dutch uncle not to do it. The sergeant found out about it, and he transferred out soon after I came back to the outfit.

Leyte was becoming pretty secure. The first calvary left. So did bunch of other troops. But our company was down on manpower because of all the bombing and strafing; we were down to around eighty men from 200.

A few had been killed like Lieutenant Bernie, but most had only been wounded from shrapnel. The army brought in six new quartermaster companies to take over what we had been doing, one company for each dump. They took the five of us off driving truck and put our company to work stacking rations. On the second night, our squad was stacking rations, but I guess some of the guys weren't doing it right or going fast enough for this new gung-ho sergeant. He began picking on Sherman C., the smallest in our bunch. Sherman C. couldn't fight his way out of a paper bag. Everyone was so pissed they slowed down to nearly a standstill, barely moving the boxes. The sarge started to raise hell about having us all court-martialed for not working. I came down off the stack where I was working and said, "Hey, sarge, there is something over here I want to show you." He came over by the stack and asked where. I said right back here. When we got between two stacks, each about twelve feet high, I grabbed him by his shirt and put my thumb knuckles against his adam's apple. I explained to him that these guys had been here from day one and that all the dumps had been run by just these few men and until he had come along expecting to crack the whip and acting like we were all a bunch of dummies. Then I explained that if he said anything about my grabbing him, it would probably be the last time he said anything about anything. The rest of the night was quieter, and so were the other nights.

I don't know what happened after that, but our outfit was no longer working for the new quartermaster company. What they did was move us from White Beach to Taclobon. We set up on a hillside overlooking a Japanese P.O.W. camp, and our company guarded the beer dump. The five of us drivers worked for a trucking company, located close to our new camp. They put me and David H. on a semi, twelve-hour shift. We had no restrictions when off-duty, and we could eat in any of the five different mess halls around the area. It all depended where we were at the time.

W.G. had some connections in town for girls. He made a deal for fifty pesos a month, a new house, and a girl anytime we wanted, so for $12.50 each, it was a good deal. The girl's name was Aning, and her father was with her. The money we gave her paid for their rent plus food. The house had two small bedrooms and a large living room and kitchen combined. Of course, their kitchen was just a place to build a fire, and the bedroom was just a mat on the floor, but for them it was a home.

Aning was a good go. She wasn't the cutest, but she knew how to use it. We would take some beer down to them and cigs and once in a while some rations. They liked the "K" rations for the chocolate.

With Aning, whoever went first, she would bathe you afterwards. When she bathed me, she would play around enough to go again, but with W.G.

she wouldn't. He always asked me why it took so long. In fact, sometimes when I wanted to leave, she would pull me back down to stay. I never did tell W.G. what she was doing or that she wanted me. I didn't want to hurt W.G.'s feelings.

Driving semi and having access to quite a few dumps made it easier to finagle things from the sergeants. I never blackmailed anyone, but I would trade a couple of T-shirts for cigars or something else for Spanish olives, etc. That way, while I was driving, I could be smoking a cigar, chewing an olive or drinking a beer.

We had to line up for our beer rations like the rest of them. But when the guys in our company got low on beer, I would back up between two stacks in the C&E dump so the guys guarding the beer dump could pass it under the fence. Those cases I would haul back down to our tents, and whoever was in camp would help unload and hide them. I am sure our commanding officer knew what was going on, but he never said a word. Our tents were right below the officers' and noncoms' tents, so backing a semi down the row couldn't help being seen and heard. But anyway, we usually had a supply of beer on hand.

The food and other supplies were coming in regularly. Being able to eat at five different mess halls, I would always try to find out which one was having the best food. Whichever was the best, I would try to be there.

One time when David H. was driving our rig, a federal four-wheel-drive cab over, he got stuck in some sand with a load and didn't know how to get out. He also couldn't figure out how to put it in front-wheel-drive. So when I came on shift and asked where my truck was, the motor pool sergeant said it was stuck down at the C&E dump with a broken axle. He said "We will run you down and see what you can do." When we got there, I saw it wasn't stuck that badly. We got some planks, put them under the trailer dollies, and cranked down the dollies so there wasn't any weight on the fifth wheel. We dug a little sand out in front of the dual tires, I got in, put it in front-wheel-drive, and drove it out. The guys around were surprised at how easy it was. I drove the tractor up to the motor pool and told the sergeant that it needed a new driver's side rear axle. The sergeant couldn't believe how I knew all of this stuff. I said, "Sarge, I was driving trucks in the woods at fourteen years old. In the spring there were a lot of mud holes, and if you went through them too fast, you would turn over. If you were too slow, you would get stuck and sometimes tear up a universal joint or maybe snap an axle. Since there would be no one to help you, you learned." I also said I had other mechanical training.

He asked "Why are you just a private?" I said, "Our company is a service company with no rank, and I don't much give a shit. I do my part and I enjoy it, or at least I make the best of it."

They did find a new axle for the tractor, and the sarge said, "From now on, you are the only one who drives it."

I asked, "Off-duty, too?" He said, "Sometimes."

One night, Brownie and I decided to go to Tacloben to find some gals. Our houseboy went along as our interpreter. It was another one of those dark nights. As we were walking down the road, we met a couple of Filipino gals. I started to talk to them. Brownie and the houseboy went on. After I left the two gals, I couldn't find Brownie. I was wondering where he went. As I was walking toward town, I heard our houseboy yell, "Hey, Esky, over here." Back off the road a little ways was a hut. The houseboy said, "Brownie is in there."

I yelled, "Hey, Brownie, you want a rubber?"

He said, "Hell no, it's too late." When he got through, he came out and said, "Why don't you go in and give it a try?" I said okay. Then Brownie said that he was going to town to get a pro, and he would see us back at camp. I went inside, and in the candlelight was this cute Filipino gal. We hugged and kissed a little, and then we were on a mat on the floor. (I didn't forget my rubber.) When I got in the saddle, I thought I was making love to a corpse. I said to myself, This has to be better than that. There was a small pillow laying off to the side. I put in under her butt, and boy, did that help.

When we were through, she was bathing me and saying, "You must stay all night."

She kept saying that until our houseboy hollered, "Esky, Esky." We heard some talking a short distance away, and she said, "You must go, my husband is coming. Hurry! Hurry!" While I was trying to get dressed and pulling my pants up, four big, black bucks came in. I thought, Oh shit! I am going to have to fight my way out of this. I backed against the wall still trying to get my pants buttoned.

One of them said, "Well, how was it, white boy?" I said it was pretty good. Then he said that was fine and that I could come back any time I wanted to, we were all over here for one purpose so we may as well enjoy ourselves.

I said thanks and left. The houseboy and I went back to camp. Brownie wasn't there yet since he had gone into Tacloben for his pro. When he got back to camp, I told him about the ordeal. He laughed and said he was glad it was me in that situation instead of him. Neither one of us went back for seconds.

Another time, I had to go into Tacloben for a load with a 6 by 6. Brownie wanted to ride along. On the way, I saw the Filipino gal I had talked to before. I stopped and asked her if she wanted to go for a ride. She got in the cab with us. I put my arm around her and was hugging her. She was also cuddling up to me. So we turned off the main road and found a place where a company had moved out but left their tents up. So I said to Brownie, "You keep guard in case anyone comes." I took the G.I. blanket off the seat, and she and I went into the tent. When we were through, we went back to the truck. I asked her to give Brownie some, but she said no, she just wanted me.

After we dropped her off, I said to Brownie, "Sorry you didn't get any."

He said, "Don't feel bad, I was watching you two all the time, and I enjoyed it as much as you did."

I had another ordeal while still at White Beach. I was walking in Tacloben when I saw this Filipino doll and struck up a conversation. She asked me if I liked fried bananas. I said I had never had them, so she invited me to her house for some. She lived alone, but she had two Filipino men as her escorts. I thought that was a little strange, but I didn't question it. She had a small house on stilts. After we had eaten the fried bananas I kissed her a couple of times. Then she said that we had better close the shutters, which we did. The kissing and petting was getting pretty heavy when all at once, there was a bunch of banging on the outside of the house. The escort were using their fists and sticks. I asked her what was going on because I couldn't understand their language. She said they wanted me out of there so they could kill me because they didn't want me to be with her. She kept begging me not to go out. I thought it over and knew I had to leave sometime. I knew I would have a better chance in the daylight than at night, so I found a bamboo stick about five long and an inch and a half around. It was the only protection I had. The house had a small, enclosed porch with steps going down. I went out on the porch and said, "I will leave and never come back, but if any of you try to get me, I will get a few of you first." There were about fourteen of them, and after some jabbering, they moved back. They had bolo knives and sticks. I didn't turn my back on them until I was out of range. I was just glad to be away from that.

All she knew about me was that my name was Esky and that I lived at White Beach, so I was surprised when about a week later one of her escorts came into camp and said Maria wanted to come to White Beach to live with me. I explained that I wanted no part of it. But I did ask what was the big deal, anyway. He explained that she was a princess from another island and some of her followers didn't want any foreigner making love to her. But she had run away from her island. I told him I would love to be with her, but all the time I was really thinking that if she could find me through their grapevine, why couldn't the others do the same. It did make me a little nervous.

One day I was eating fried chicken at one of the mess halls when a lieutenant came in and told me to grab some extra chicken because we had an emergency run. He told me to go to the ordinance depot and pick up a load, then to the Tanawan airstrip, where a C-47 was waiting. I was to hurry. There would be no speed limit, and there would be M.P.s at all the major intersections. All I needed was to have my lights on because most of them knew my truck anyway. He also said that when I got to the airfield, there would be a jeep waiting to escort me to the plane.

I thought to myself, Boy this is great, no speed limit, so I backed up to the dock at the depot. I was going to help them load, but they said, "Just go back to your cab and eat your chicken."

I thought, Wow, this is great. When I pulled ahead to close the trailer doors, I looked in and said, "Is that all you are putting in there?" They informed me that it was enough. To me, it looked like five-gallon acid containers in glass with a crate for each one. They had them blocked off so they wouldn't shift. They also told me to get to Tanawan as fast as I could, so away I went. When I passed an M.P., he would wave me on and give me a highball sign. It was about a forty-mile drive from where I started.

When I got to the airport and backed up to the plane so they could unload, the pilot said to me, "Well I see you made it."

When I said, "What do you mean, 'See you made it'?"

He asked, "Do you know what you have on your trailer?" I said it looked like acid, but he informed me that I had 2000 pounds of nitroglycerin. I started to think about all the bumps I hit and got kind of shaky. But then, if I knew what I was hauling, I would have been too careful and blown myself up anyhow. But after that, I always made it a point to know what I was hauling.

One of our loading and unloading docks was right downtown in Tacloben, and right beside the dock was a whorehouse. There were over twenty gals there, so sometimes when I would have to wait for a load to come in from a ship, I would go into the whorehouse and have a beer. I got to know the owner pretty well, and he always wanted me to take one of his girls. I told him, why should I pay for it when I could get it free? I would give him a handful of cigars now and then or take in a jar of olives, and he and I would sit, drink, eat olives, and smoke. It got to the point where he wouldn't charge me for a drink, and since he could speak English pretty well, we could B.S. with each other.

One day Brownie and I were waiting for a load to come in when a new girl came in to work in the house. The boss said, "Go ahead, Esky, try her out and see how good she is, no charge." We fooled around a little before we got started. When we were through another guy wanted to take her on. She came over, grabbed me, and told the boss that all she wanted was a souvenir from me, a baby. The boss said, "Well, Esky, I guess it's up to you." I saw her every other day, but after two weeks, she just up and left. I guess she got what she wanted.

My dad was pretty sick when I was at Tacloben. I had letters from three different doctors that told me he had about thirty days to live. I took the letters to the Red Cross, but they said it wasn't enough evidence to have me go home. I was a necessity because I was a truck driver. My dad did die thirty days later in the middle of August 1945. I asked our motor pool sergeant if I could have a few days off. I told him, "You know where to find me if you need me." He said okay, so I dropped my trailer, took the tractor, and parked it down by the loading dock.

The owner of the whorehouse knew about my situation, so when I asked if I could stay there for a few days, he said no problem. It was just like a harem, plenty to eat and drink, and plenty of girls. Some would be singing to me and some bathing me, all at the same time. There were always five or six girls around. When customers came in, I would either sleep or go sit at the bar. Since there was a 11:00 P.M. curfew, the M.P.s would go around with the boss checking to see that there weren't any G.I.s hanging around. When they came come to the room I was in, the M.P.s would ask, "Who is in there?"

The boss would say in a low voice, "Sh-sh-sh, it's one of your M.P.s." They would just go on then. On the evening of the fifth day, the sergeant sent word down that I was needed, so the next morning I was ready to go. I thanked the boss and took off. Of course, I would still stop by every once in a while, like before.

Aning was with W.B. at the house we rented for her. Then one day at Aning's, her cousin, Tausing, came over. We visited some, then she asked me to walk her home. Aning threw a fit, but I did anyway. Tausing was younger, and I didn't have to pay any rent.

Her place was further across town and there wasn't anyplace to park my truck because the streets were narrow and the huts were close together, so when it was time for me to go to work, one of the other drivers would drive down the street. When he got near the house, he would gun the motor three times, go down the road, and come back in ten minutes. I would be waiting. David H. and Early were driving the 6 by 6 and if they weren't around by forty-five minutes before quitting time, I would have to go after them. They had some girls that lived in a hut out in a rice paddy away from the road. David and Early didn't like to walk the rice paddies, especially at night, so they would drive their trucks as far as they could into the paddy. I would then have to winch them out so they could get back to the motor pool.

At the loading docks, I met Dallas L. He was driving for a refrigeration company. We would haul frozen food or fresh fruit when we would get it to store in their frozen lockers or cold storage. My van or trailer wasn't a refrigerated one, but Dallas' outfit had about six of the refrigerated trailers. Unfortunately, he didn't have the leniency I did with his tractor. In the frozen food storage, we would cut the top off G.I. water cans and fill them with water. That gave us ice, which was a rarity on the islands. When we moved to Tacloben from White Beach, we lost all our refrigerator vans. Anyway once a week, our squad would have a beer bust in our tent (cold beer). We would get my monkey, "Pissed Off," drunk also. He was a small monkey that could sit in the palm of your hand. He was hilarious when half drunk. One day Dallas and I heard there was a ship out in the harbor with stateside whiskey. So Dallas came up with the idea of swiping his company commander's duck, going out into the bay, and getting some. We had to wait until things settled down around his company. We got the duck, and as we were driving through the narrow streets, I saw some headlights coming over this hill really fast. I said to Dallas, "That S.O.B. is going to broadside us."

Dallas laughed and said, "Oh well, we have the right-of-way because we are on a through street." It got closer, and we could see it was a jeep by the headlights. The jeep didn't stop until it hit the duck just behind the rear wheels. We jumped off the duck to see if anyone was hurt in the jeep. There were two officers and two nurses in the jeep, and they were getting out. They were dazed as well as being half-loaded.

We asked if anyone was hurt, and all the lieutenant that was driving kept saying was "You aren't going to report us, are you?" We didn't answer him. Dallas was looking at the damage. I saw one nurse staggering around. I went over and put my arms around her asking if she was all right.

She said that she was a little weak and dizzy, so I said, "Let me hold you up." In the meantime, Dallas and the two officers were looking at an eight-inch hole they had knocked into the duck. It had bent the bumper on the jeep but they could still drive it. The other nurse was just standing there. I put my hand on the breast of the nurse I was holding up, and to my surprise, she didn't resist. Instead, she put her arms around me and gave me a good kiss. That broke the ice. I asked her name and told her mine was Esbibbie, but they called me Esky for short. She thought that was funny. By this time, the officer that she was with was beginning to listen to our conversation. I was just about to find out how to get in touch with her when he told her to shut up, an officer (nurse) couldn't date enlisted men.

Well no one reported the accident because we had borrowed the duck and the damage wasn't too bad. Then Dallas and I decided not to take it out in the bay after all. We took it back to the original place. A few days later, we decided to look it over. Nothing was done to the hole, so we started it up. It was then we found out that the bilge pump wasn't working. If we had taken it out in the bay after the accident, we would have sunk for sure. Luck was on our side that day.

It was the first part of August when we found out the war was over. Dallas and I were downtown in Tacloben in an upstairs bar and dance hall where we went once in a while. It was really off-limits for G.I.s, but it was early evening, just late enough to be dark. Dallas and I had just left this joint and were heading for another. We got onto the street when a weapons carrier pulled up with a load of M.P.s. Some of them ran upstairs, broke open the door, and yelled, "It's all over." Dallas and I thought, Boy we got out of there just in time to keep from getting caught in a raid. Then a couple of M.P.s grabbed Dallas and me and said again, "It's all over."

We said, "We didn't do anything, we were just walking down the street." They held onto us, dancing around us, and just repeating it was all over! Finally we got it out of them that the war was over. Only a short time later, the ship's foghorns started blowing. Air raid sirens were going off, and the big guns on the ship were even firing a few volleys.

Dallas and I decided to get a jug of whiskey to celebrate, so we went to the place close to our company. We ran most of the way because it was closer to walk there than to take a truck, and we wanted to beat the crowd. When we got there, most of our company was there plus some others. The stairs up to the liquor store ran up along one wall. Dallas and I were waiting in line standing on the stairs when above us we heard "Hey, Esky, you want some whiskey?"

I said "Sure!"

So one of the guys from camp handed me two gallons out the window and said, "Take one for me." We took off and gave our friend his gallon. Then we decided to go and get my semi. We got some beer and took Jack S. with us.

We got in a line of bumper-to-bumper traffic. We didn't know where the lead trucks were going, but my rig was empty so I said to Dallas and Jack, "Watch this." I set the air; it didn't slow me up at all. The tires were just sliding, so then I started pushing. When we got a chance to get out of the string, we did. We finally took a nap about 10 A.M. the next day.

A couple of days later, things settled down some and we were back hauling, just like normal.

I was hauling fresh eggs to cold storage one day for distribution. Dallas was also hauling with his rig. since I was the last one to get a load, the sarge said, "Okay take off."

It was just a few crates of eggs, so I asked, "What am I supposed to do with them?"

The sarge said, "I don't give a damn what you do with them, just get them out of here." Since there wasn't any paperwork on them and since Dallas was already gone, I went to his outfit and told him the deal, if we were going to keep those eggs, we would have to swap trailers, because mine wasn't refrigerated. So we transferred the twenty-seven crates of eggs. I think that this was the first time there were fresh eggs on the island for the troops. The only other fresh eggs were what you could get from the natives, usually already cooked and served in cafes. Dallas and I were already wondering what we were going to do with twenty-seven crates of eggs. We went to our native buddy who ran the whorehouse and traded a couple of crates for some whiskey. The whiskey was in beer bottles. Now we had to get something to mix with it. We went to my outfit and talked to the mess sergeant. He traded three crates for a couple of cases of canned orange juice. Then we found Jack S. and asked if he wanted to go along.

He asked if there was booze, and then he said, "Hell, yes." We went back to Dallas' outfit and traded three crates for a couple of cases of canned grapefruit juice. We also got ice from them. At another outfit, we traded for tomato juice, Tabasco sauce, and Worcestershire sauce. We had salt and pepper already. So we were having mixed drinks and driving around.

While driving around, I said to Jack and Dallas that all the time we had been over there, we had never made a WAC. "Let's go to the WAC area and get that mess sergeant. We can trade a crate of eggs for a piece of tail." We all agreed. The WAC area was set off the road about a block, and it was just a jeep trail going into it since most of the officers who dated WACs had jeeps.

Anyway, we were half-loaded as I drove my semi down the jeep trail to the WAC area. They had a high fence around the whole area with M.P. guards out front. When we pulled in, the M.P. asked what we wanted. I said I would like to see the mess sergeant. The M.P. went to locate her. He came back out and said she wasn't in. I then asked for the assistant. He went in and came back out with this WAC who wasn't bad-looking. Her name was Mickey. We walked over into a guest hut just outside of the fence, and I put the deal to her. I asked if they had had any fresh eggs while they had been there, and she said no. Then I said that we had some to trade, but the deal would be one crate for one romp in the woods. I also said that she might even get another stripe for getting the eggs, but she kept saying that she couldn't do that. So I told her to come over and have a drink anyway. It was a hot, muggy night, and the refer was running full blast with the back doors open, so it felt pretty good. There were some extra canteen cups in the guest hut. It was a thatched hut of fairly good size. They had two of them, maybe twenty feet apart. We got the extra canteen cups, and she agreed to have a drink with us, but that was all. I explained that we weren't bad guys, we were just out for a good time. I also explained that our drinks were good rice whiskey mixed with any type of juice she wanted. The whiskey and juices were setting against the cooling coils in the refer, poured over the ice, it was delicious. There were a couple more WACs who came out for a drink and to see who the crazy fool was to drive a semi on the jeep trail. Jack, Dallas, and I were taking turns serving drinks, but when I wasn't pouring for someone, I was over by Mickey talking to her. We were giving her pretty stiff drinks. After a few drinks I got her up by the front of the trailer and asked if she would like to sit in the driver's seat. She said yes, and we climbed up. She thought that was pretty great. When she was getting out, she had to jump a little, so I helped her, and when she landed I gave her a good kiss. It sort of surprised her, but she also liked it. We started smooching between the trac- tor and the trailer then. I was doing a little caressing and things were getting better when I asked her if she still wanted the eggs. To my surprise, she said, "Oh, what the hell." So we went in the bushes. I carried in a crate of eggs. The M.P. on duty had to go along as an escort. Then Jack disappeared, and there went another crate of eggs. The M.P. was getting quite a kick out of our dealings. After the third time, we gave an extra crate for good measure.

When the dealing was over, we all were still drinking. The other WACs were coming in from their dates by then, because they had to be in by 11:00 P.M.. Some checked in, then came back out for a few drinks. We were also supposed to be out of there by 11:00 P.M.. At midnight we were still there having quite a party with a dozen or so drinking. The M.P.s had a midnight change of shift, but the one who was enjoying the whole merry-go-round said he wanted to stay and see how we were going to get this rig out of there. He also asked if we would take him back to his outfit. We found out where it was, and since it wasn't too far out of our way, we said sure, but he would have to hang on the side or ride in the back of the cab, between the tractor and the trailer. He said that was fine with him. In a cab over, as it was called, there are two seats with the gearshift between them. With Jack and Dallas sitting on each other's lap, there wasn't room for anyone else inside the cab. We were giving the M.P. a few drinks extra for him to catch up, but the party was slowing down. Mickey was one of the last to leave. I sort of latched onto her because she seemed pretty nice. Jack S. was up in the trailer mixing drinks. When he got through, he came to the back of the trailer where Dallas was standing with his back to the open doors and a drink in hand. Of course, Jack also had a drink in his hand. Jack climbed on Dallas's shoulders with his legs over the front and said, "Giddy up, giddy up," and acted like he was spurring Dallas. Dallas took one step, and they both went face first in the grass and mud. Jack got up, and Dallas was trying to get up when Jack said, "Goddamn you Dallas, you never do anything right." Everyone just split laughing.

Finally, at 1:30 A.M., we decided to leave. I had to back the trailer sharply on the blind side between the two guest houses. The other reason for the close quarters was that there were Filipino huts all around. I had plenty of help, some saying hold it, others saying okay, depending on what side of the trailer they were on. The M.P. was hanging on the outside on the passenger side, and after I had backed up far, I started to go ahead. I knew I was close to one hut, but the M.P. that was hanging on the side swung himself behind the cab between the tractor and the trailer and said, "Go ahead, you can make it." Well, we took out one of the stilts holding up a corner of the hut, and down it came. But we didn't stop. We took the M.P. to his outfit and gave him a couple of crates of eggs. The rest of the eggs we split between Dallas' outfit and ours.

I was still shacking up with Tausing, and W.G. was with Aning. We were also going down to see the owner of the whorehouse when our company got orders to send a platoon of men to Luson. Of course it was our platoon that was going. But seeing that the war was over and there was more going on up there, we hoped they had stateside whiskey we could buy. We were supposed to debark at Orange Beach at 10:00 a.m., so with a few trucks loaded with our equipment, we were there waiting to go. I wasn't driving for a change. The platoon in our section came to see us off. They were bringing beer and whiskey to us on the beach while we were waiting for a LST. They were running back and forth for more beer, so we got rid of our gas masks and put beer in the holder so we could have some on the way up to Luson. With all the whiskey and everything it was one hell of a big party. I was pretty loaded when the LST came in for us to load. Our lieutenant asked me, "Esky, do you want me to carry your duffel bag on board?"

Of course, being half-loaded, I said. "I don't need any officer to carry my duffel bag." He said it was time to go. I was sitting down leaning on something, so I got up. I was walking up and down the beach looking for my duffel bag.

The lieutenant yelled, "Esky, your duffel bag is over here." I went over, got it, put it over my shoulder, and thanked him. Then he said, "Do you know that you were leaning on your bag all the time you were sitting there?" I felt like a fool.

We boarded around 10:00 P.M.. We had been partying for twelve hours and had some sandwiches. So the five of us from the old gang made a bet. The first one to get seasick had to buy a fifth of stateside whiskey. I have a strong stomach, but.... When we got into the China Sea, we were in a complete blackout. It was so dark that you couldn't see your hand in front of your face, so we all were rolled up in our G.I. blankets, sleeping on the open deck. I was crawling over some guys trying to get to the rail but when I got there, I had to wedge myself between a couple of guys already there losing their cookies. We were there until daybreak came, and I found out that of the five guys that made the bet, I was the last one. Earl R. from Texas was the first to the rail, but it was quite a while before we found some stateside whiskey.

We wound up about eighty miles north of Manila, twelve miles southeast of Tarlac. We set up our tents about thirty feet from a liquor store. The Spaniards had a distillery close to where the motor pool was set up, so everything was pretty handy, and our commanding officer and one other officer were in command. Our commanding officer was a captain, and the other was a first lieutenant. Our motor pool sergeant we nicknamed Stew. He was with the company on Leyte.

About three days later, they blew the assembly bugle, so we all fell out and assembled. Our captain came out and said "I am sure you all are wondering what we are doing here. Well, I will tell you. We are farmers!" We all shouted, "Farmers?" And then we looked at each other and started to laugh. After he quieted us back down, he explained that we were going to raise fresh produce for the troops. He then asked who could drive a quick-way crane, but no one put their hand up. Finally, I said I could drive anything.

So Stew took five of us down to base "X" in Manila to see General Seabrook, a big farmer in New York state. I am sure you have heard of the Seabrook Farms. When the orderly asked Stew who wanted to see the general, he told the orderly, "Just the farmers."

The orderly looked dumbfounded, but when he told the general, he hollered out, "Come on in, you Goddamned farmers." The orderly about crapped his pants. The general gave us a requisition for one quick-way thirty-five ton truck and four six by six trucks. Everything was new. I couldn't go as fast as the others, so one truck stayed with me while the rest went on. The farm machinery started to come in. I had to learn to operate the crane, but it didn't take long. After about a week of uncrating and assembling machinery, they spotted some flatcars on a narrow- gauge track with some D-2 Cats, D-4 Cats, and some R-2s. There were about sixteen of them, but once again, no one knew how to run a Cat. I said, "Hell, that is right down my line." The siding where they spotted the flatcars was about three-fourths of a mile from the motor pool, and a set of tracks ran right into the distillery. The distillery even had a little engine sitting there. So I asked the sarge if we could fire up the engine to bring the flatcars in to unload.

He asked, "You mean you know how to run an engine, too?"

I said, "Not really, but I bet I can make it go." I remembered back when I was a kid and thrashing season came around with steam tractors pulling the thrashing machines. They took a long belt off a pulley, and then they would do the thrashing. I helped a few times to thrash. I would be the fireman, keeping enough wood in the firebox to keep the steam at a certain pressure as well as watching the water level. We checked over the engine to see if there were any bullet holes in it or if anything had rusted out too badly, but it looked pretty good. So we got a bunch of sugarcane stalks and hauled water like mad. We filled the boiler to a happy medium and built a fire. It wasn't long before the steam gauge started to rise. When it got up to forty pounds, Earl R. just had to try the whistle. It wasn't too loud, but the guys in the motor pool came out and cheered. So did some of the distillery workers. They said the engine hadn't been used since the Japanese came. Some of the guys were ringing the bell. We finally got the steam up a little higher, and old engineer Esky released the brake, slowly moving the throttle forward. There were some squeaks and groans, but finally we were moving. We really had to watch all the switches, but we didn't know to much about them. With all the help, we made it, of course. Everyone wanted to ride, and it took lots of cane stalk to keep the steam up. After that the Spaniards and the motor pool used it every once in a while.

To unload the Cats, there wasn't anyplace to off-load, so we built a small ramp, but it was still a drop-off of at least two feet. So, after we took the off the blocking that was holding up the blades, we would start it up, put it in low gear, head it in the right direction, jump off, and let it go. Getting back on was quite a snap when the back of the Cat-tracks came of the flat car.

After we took the blocking off one of the Cats, we could not get the blade to come down. We even tried jumping on it. So I said, "Maybe there's too much hydraulic fluid in it. Let's take this plug off and try." The plug was horizontal on the cylinder. There was a lieutenant there from base "X" watching us unload. He was standing about thirty feet away while we were trying to get this blade down. Earl R., Art T., and I were jumping on it finally when it broke loose. The hydraulic fluid shot out like a bullet and hit the lieutenant right in the middle of the chest. I guess he thought he was shot. He staggered back a little, gave us a dirty look, and walked off. He never said a word.

We had some coconut palms near our company area. Stew wondered how we were going to get them out with the Cat. I had to show them how; make a few passes on each side and then the opposite of whichever way you want it to fall, then get the blade under the ball of roots and lift. If we had a larger Cat, we could have just dropped the blade, dug down, and lifted, making it in one pass.

Seeing that I was the only Cat skinner they had, they wanted me to teach the others and work in the fields. I couldn't see being out there eight to ten hours a day working in a field when I could have the Manila run with fresh produce and not be so confined, so I told our captain that I would teach our guys for a week. By that time they should have enough experience to teach the others. Earl R. also took the Manila run, so we were the only two steady Manila drivers.

The base "X" farmers grew tomatoes, bell peppers, radishes, green onions, yams, and sweet potatoes. Other potatoes would rot. They had to plant twice as many tomatoes and peppers because the natives would swipe them. They didn't bother the radishes or onions too much. We even had to haul pipe for irrigation because it was the dry season. We would go to Clark Field for rations. It wasn't very long before we were hauling a couple truckloads two or three times a week to the San Miguel Brewery in Manila, where they had cold storage for distribution. And if we needed anything either, I or Earl R. would go into base "X" to see General Seabrook. When he knew we were in the orderly room, he would yell, "Come on in, you Goddamned farmers." We go to know each other really well, and we were his pet project, so the boys could always get some fresh vegetables.

When the general wanted a break, he would come up to the farm. We had a covered mess hall, but we also had tables outside if the weather was nice. When the general came up, he would bring a few bottles of stateside whiskey. If our officers wanted to eat with the general, they would have to come outside to eat with us since that was where the general would be. He would set a bottle or two of whiskey on the table while we were eating.

It wasn't that we didn't have enough booze, because the Spanish guy that owned the distillery gave most of the guys free whiskey. The motor pool would do some welding for him, and I would do some hauling for him. Earl R. and I would be invited over to his home to eat. They were really nice people. Sometimes the distillery owner, Philip, would throw a party at his large, Spanish-style home. His wife was good-looking, and his wife's sister, nicknamed Sunshine, was also good-looking. Sunshine had her own little cottage out behind their home. She shacked up mostly with officers from around the area. Of course we peons couldn't afford her anyway.

There was a little barrio up the road about three-fourths of a mile, with three whorehouses, a couple of cafes, barber shops, and grocery stores with very little in them. One hooker called herself the B-29. She was a big Filipino. I mean good-sized. Then there was another who was young and trim and who called herself P-38. She would say she could outmaneuver the B-29. But the B-29 had the most business because she was good. When we didn't make the Manila run, I would go to the barrio in the early afternoon to beat the rush. She knew that I was going to Manila pretty regularly, so she asked me if I could get some lipstick and rouge. I did get some through a couple of WACs at base "X," so I didn't have to pay anymore. After that, I kept her supplied with goodies. One afternoon when we were finished, I started to get dressed. She said, "Where are you going, honey? There is plenty of time yet." She said she enjoys it with me, but at night there wasn't any enjoyment. So I became her so-called lover.

Only Earl R. knew what was going on, and sometimes when the guys would be heading to the base, they would ask, "Hey, Esky, aren't you going out tonight?" I would just say that I wasn't in the mood, not saying that I was pooped out.

Then there was Helen, who worked at the little cafe. After the cafe closed, we would go into the backroom. We would kiss and caress. Both of us would get hot, but she wouldn't let me do it unless we were married by a priest, so I was just her kissing lover.

Then one day, the P-38 invited me over. When I got in the saddle with her, there wasn't any maneuvering. But when she reached over, got an apple, and started eating it, that did it. It hurt my ego, so I went back to the B-29.

Once in a while I would be able to get a weapon-carrier and go into Tarlac. There I met another cute waitress. I didn't get to see her very often. She was like Helen, just the kissing and petting type.

Well with only forty of us now doing our job, there wasn't any reveille or retreat. We all got along fine and did our job. Then one day, 120 new men with a new commanding officer arrived because our old captain was ready to go home. We now had two new second lieutenants while our new commanding officer was a first lieutenant.

In a week, our good captain was gone. The day after he left, there was a weird sound in the air early in the morning. It was the bugler was blowing reveille. All the new recruits got dressed and fell in line, while in our four tents, there wasn't any movement. The new commanding officers came around and gave each one of us a direct order to fall in. This went on for two mornings. On the third day, he called for an assembly of the old 969 quartermaster bunch. When we assembled, we didn't line up and cover down. We just stood there in a group. Our new first lieutenant started telling us how he was going to make soldiers out of us if it was the last thing he did. Then he said that if we would play ball with him, he would play ball with us. That was when Earl R. with his slow Texas drawl said, "Yep, you do all the pitching and we do all the catching." Everybody busted out laughing. The lieutenant yelled back saying that will be enough of that and throwing his fist in the air.

He tried reveille again but it was the same thing. So he decided to wait until all of the older guys went home before he started making soldiers out of the rest. On the point system, we were pretty high, but the new lieutenant put a curfew in effect of 11:00 P.M. lights out and in bed. During this time, a couple more cafes opened up closer to our camp. Well, our new commander was going to make sure the curfew was enforced, so he and the company orderly would ride around at night to see if they could find anyone. We called our company orderly Connie because he acted sort of sissy-like, but his real name was Conrad. Anyway one night I was walking back to camp around 11:15 P.M. I was not on the regular road but walking on a parallel road. Here came a jeep, but I didn't think anything of it. So they drove up to me, and Connie asked me what I was doing out so late. I said I was looking for a piece of ass but couldn't find any, so I was heading back to camp. Well our new commander had me report to him the first thing in the morning.

The next morning I was supposed to take seven guys to Manila in the weapons carrier to pick up some new trucks. None of us older bunch kept our shirttails tucked in or our shirts buttoned. Lots of the time, we didn't even wear a shirt. So when I walked into his office, my shirttail was out and my shirt unbuttoned. I walked in, gave a salute, and said, "Private Diemel reporting as ordered, sir."

He said, "What do you mean coming in here dressed like that? Button up that shirt and stick your shirttail in."

I said, "Yes, sir," stepped back, and proceeded to follow the order. After I got through, I stepped forward and said, "Now, what do you want?"

He noticed I had a civilian belt on, one that a Filipino had made for me, so of course he then asked, "What are you doing with that civilian belt on?"

I said, "You know, sir, that mine is in the laundry, and I have to have something to hold my pants up." He came back with a remark that I had to be a better soldier than to have only one belt, and I answered that I was a damned good soldier. He then proceeded to give me company punishment for breaking curfew of three days restriction to the company area from 5 P.M. until 10:45 P.M. I would have to sign in every fifteen minutes at the orderly room. I said, "Is that all, sir?"

He said, "Yes."

Then I said, "I guess I better go. He then told me that I wasn't going anywhere until he said it is okay for me to leave, so I leaned my butt against his desk, folded my arms, and told him that there were seven men waiting for me to take them to Manila, but I guess that didn't make any difference. After about ten minutes of silence, he said that I could go. I thanked him and walked out without saluting. I thought that he might call me back, but he didn't. I told the guys what had happened, and after that the old guys gave him the cold shoulder.

When he said something, they would just say, "Yes, sir." I didn't find out the guys had done that until much later.

Well, I went over to the orderly room with my pen and paper and finally got caught up on some letter-writing. Then a couple of my buddies brought Helen down so we could go out in back and do a little necking. I would come back in and sign my name and time then go back out. After my company punishment, he relaxed on the curfew.

One day the commander called me into his office and said to me, "I see that you are pretty well-liked by most of the men." He went and explained how they hardly spoke to him after my company restriction. He then offered that if I would re-enlist for six months, he would make me first sergeant because the old first sergeant was going home in a week. I told him that I appreciated the offer, but I preferred to go home. He then asked me what he had to do to get the men to speak to him again. I said that it was not for me to tell an officer what to do, but I would talk to some of the men. I also explained that General Seabrook said we were just a bunch of farmers, but he liked to come up here to relax, and that we didn't need all the military bull. I mentioned the way the general acted when he did come up, just being one of the boys.

Well I sent word through the grapevine to ease off on the cold shoulder, and our new lieutenant turned out to be a fairly decent guy. He even let me use his personal jeep to go to Tarlac once in a while.

Our old officer from the motor pool went home, and we got a new ninety-day wonder. He was going to change things just to show his authority. Now we weren't supposed to do anything for the distillery, and we weren't supposed to come into the motor pool garage. The first time I had a little conflict with him was when Earl R., Art T., and I were over in Talac in a bar. I was dancing with my part-time girlfriend when he came in and tried to take her away from me. After a dance, he would call her over to his table and have her stay there. She would look at me, but all I could do was shrug my shoulders because I didn't want to get into trouble. After that night, he told the motor pool sergeant that I couldn't have any off-duty vehicles. He figured that way I wouldn't be running any competition with him. When I knew he was going to Tarlac, I went to our commanding officer and told him that our second lieutenant wouldn't let me have a vehicle to go to Tarlac, but that I wanted to go and see my girlfriend. He said, "Here, take mine. I am not going to use it tonight." So when I went into the bar, Maria was with the second lieutenant but when she saw me, she came running over and gave me a big kiss.

Then she came over and sat with me. The lieutenant called me over and said, "Why don't you go down the street to another bar to do your drinking." I told him that I liked it here. He said he would give me five dollars if I left. After refusing the five dollars, he offered me ten dollars. I told him that he could go down the street if he wanted to. Then I took Maria home. The next day the good second lieutenant gave the order that when Earl R. and I were not going to Manila, we would have to work in the fields.

Shortly after that, General Seabrook came up. After we had a chow with him, about six of us were walking down the road talking about different things. He wondered how the officers were getting along. We said the commander was okay, but then we told the general that the new second lieutenant wasn't getting along too well. I explained the things he was doing and told him he could talk to Stew, the motor pool sarge, about what the second lieutenant was doing. The general didn't say any more about it, but less than a week later the lieutenant was transferred out of our outfit. He never was replaced, that I knew of. Earl R. and I didn't have to work in the fields anymore. And on the days that we didn't go to Manila, I could visit B-29 and Helen. I never did get into Helen's pants, even when I B.S.ed her that I had signed up for six more months. She said she wanted to marry me through a priest, but I got cold feet.

I did get to sleep with Sunshine a couple of times, and we would go dancing together. Some of the new guys were a little jealous because she wouldn't go with them. One night we were dancing when one of the guys started popping off. "How much are you paying the whore, Esky, and is she was worth it?" I told him to shut up and leave us alone. Of course, he asked, "Who is big enough to make me?" One short jab to the mouth shut him up. Blood flew as he wilted. His buddies helped him out of the bar, but he kept shouting that he was going to kill me. After I left Sunshine that night around 2 A.M., I quietly went to his tent and woke him up. I told him to get up. We would go outside to see if he was going to kill me or not. He wouldn't get out of bed, but he didn't spout off anymore either.

One night Sherman, Earl R., George, and I were walking home from the barrio. It was pitch black out. We knew that we were getting close to a narrow, one-way bridge over an irrigation ditch, but we couldn't see it. I took out my zippo cigarette lighter, and just as I lit it, Sherman disappeared. He had fallen into the muddy ditch. We had to help him out because the banks were so slick. He was spitting and cussing at the same time, and he was the only one that didn't think it was funny. About the middle of December was when most of the old bunch was eligible to go home, so we were taken to a camp in Manila. We played cards and smoked moldy cigarettes while waiting to go home. With nothing to do, I made a "bingo stick" (that was what my pa called it). It is a small stick about fourteen inches long with four sides. It tapers to a round handle and has a little propeller on the end. On one of the edges, you put a bunch of notches. Then you rub it with a short stick and the propeller turns. You keep rubbing it, and it turns the other way. You give a big spiel that this is a special wood and that it understands when you talk to it. You say it came from San Mingo Island in the Pacific, the only place where they might get it to go one way. They would be talking to it, but I would tell them that they weren't talking to it right. They would try everything.

The tent we were in filled up when we came down, and the tents next to us had blacks in them, but there were some empty cots in there. So Brownie went in their tent so he could be close to the rest of us. They were a pretty good bunch. I would go in there with the bingo stick and show them how it works by talking to it. I would ask them if they would like to try, but they would say, "No, sah! That's a voodoo stick." They wouldn't touch it. I took Brownie to the side and showed him how to do it. Then he would tell the black guys that there was nothing wrong with the stick, all you had to do was talk to it. I would leave the bingo stick with Brownie and he would leave it on his cot all day, come back later, and the stick would still be in the same place. They wouldn't touch it. Then they also got thinking that there was something wrong with Brownie and me. It was pretty funny.

Word was sent down to us that they were having a Christmas Eve party and we were invited. So five of us hitchhiked up to our old outfit. The party was at a Spanish-type home with a large living room that had booths and tables. I guess at one time they had used it for a cafe. It was located about three miles from our old company, but there were enough vehicles around, so no one had to walk. They brought in a bunch of Filipino gals. Sunshine was there, along with the people from the distillery. General Seabrook had a six by six load of Seagrams 7 sent up. It was full to the sideboards. The party started about 4:00 P.M., the girls came around 6:00 P.M., there was a record player for music, and there were a bunch of snacks. Art T. and I had a booth and a couple of gals, but everyone was dancing with different gals, just a good party. The general was having a ball. Brownie was having a good time, too, but he got to feeling a little perky, so every time the general would be dancing with a gal, Brownie would go and cut in on him. Finally the general came over to me and said, "Esky, could you get your buddy Brownie to leave me alone and not cut in all the time, because I am trying to get a girl for myself tonight." So I told Brownie what he said, and Brownie left him alone because he knew the general was a great guy.

I had a dance with Sunshine and I asked her if she had a date. She said she did. Then I asked her, "How about breaking it and going with the general?" She thought that maybe the general wouldn't want her because he was quite a bit older. I said I didn't think so but I got the general off to the side and asked him if he would like to shack up with Sunshine for the night. The general knew who Sunshine was but had never had the occasion to meet her.

He said, "Would I," with a big smile, so I introduced the two of them, and that took care of that. It was probably around 2:00 A.M. when the general and Sunshine disappeared. It was 6:00 A.M. just before daylight when the party started to break up. The girls were leaving, and the only loving most of us had gotten was on the dance floor kissing. But we did have a good time. Our friend, Philip, invited us to his house because we didn't have a place to stay. We slept on their floor for about four hours before he came around with a bottle of whiskey and a beer. He said it was very necessary that we have a drink. We stared at him. His wife had a statue of Christ and a place to set candles on. The statue was about four feet high on a stand. Anyway Philip took the candles off and set the Seagrams 7 bottles in their place. His wife was a little pissed off, but she didn't say too much. She gave us some fruit for breakfast.

About noon, the general and Sunshine came in. He had a bite to eat and said that he had to get back to Manila. We had a few drinks together, shot the bull some, and then the general got me off to the side and thanked me for helping him out. Of course, we all thanked him for the good time. The general left about 2:00 P.M. and then Philip pops up and says it was very necessary that we have a nap. So we all lay down on the floor and slept for an hour or so. We ate supper at camp that night and partied at Philip's house until about midnight. We were all so tired that we just slept until morning. We had breakfast at camp, and told everyone good-bye. They hauled us to the main road, and we hitchhiked back to Manila.

It was the latter part of January 1946 when we finally got on a small aircraft carrier to come home. We played cribbage by a gun turret. I took care of a sergeant that I didn't even know. He was so seasick and weak that he could hardly move. I would take him some food and drink down in the hold and dump his throw-up. I felt sorry for him.

We came back to Camp Stoneman again in California. We were so happy to see the Golden Gate that we all gave a salute and cried a little. At Stoneman when we were lining up for chow there were a bunch of German P.O.W.s. They had big P.O.W. painted on the back of their fatigue jackets. We couldn't figure out what they were doing there serving us chow. We thought that they might poison us, so we wouldn't eat. There were probably 300 of us just standing around. Finally, a captain came out and asked what was wrong. We all pointed to the P.O.W.s, but he said it was okay. We still wouldn't go. Finally, the captain went in the line where they served and took a sample of most of the food to show us it was okay. Then we went through. The food was pretty good. We even got fresh milk. It was the first time we had fresh milk in about two years, and it sure tasted good.

From there we all went our separate ways. I wasn't the only one from Wisconsin in our outfit, so when we left Stoneman, there were two or three railroad coaches of us heading for Camp McCoy, Wisconsin. Every time the train stopped for coal, we would all get off and head for a grocery store to get milk. The shelves would be empty in no time at all. A few times the locals would yell at us and say, "That isn't a bar, the bar is over here." We would answer thanks but keep on going for the store.

I was discharged from Camp McCoy on February 13, 1946. I stopped by to see some friends on the way home and got home by bus on February 15. When I got home, I said, "Your wandering boy has returned." C.J. was also back from the service, but some of the guys had gotten killed.

Anyway, the next day I wanted to buy some clothes but we didn't have a car. Bill, the guys I used to drive for, was boarding at the tavern, and he had a Chevy pickup. He said that I could use his pickup, so off to Antigo I went. I bought shoes, jacket, scarf, pants, etc. There was a bar close to the railroad depot that I used to go to before I went into the service, and as I was getting out of the truck to go get a drink, I looked toward the passenger train at the station, and there stood my brother-in-law. I hollered, "Shorty!" and ran over there. We gave each other a hug and I told him he may as well ride home with me. (He would have gotten to Summit Lake sooner if he stayed on the train.) We stopped at a few bars on the way home. All the drinks were free. We even went on some county roads and came into Summit Lake from a different direction. His wife, (my sister, Lil), was home with a broken leg from a car accident. They sure were surprised to see Shorty with me. We got home around suppertime. Then I heard that there was a dance at the American Legion in Elcho. I asked Bill if I could use the truck again to go to Elcho. He said to me, "Hell, you had it all day, you may as well have it all night," so off I went. I put on a pair of loafers, my yellow scarf, and a sports jacket. I didn't wear a tie, though. I had to run every time I got into or out of the pickup because it was pretty cold and I didn't have a heavy coat. At the dance, the girls I used to know had dates or were married, but I was still having a good time. Some gal liked my scarf, so I lost that, and when I decided to go home I had to climb over a snowbank to get to the truck. My foot broke through the snow, and I lost one loafer. It was too cold to dig for it, so it wasn't really a good trip for me.

I checked about some of the gals I had been with before, but some had moved away while others had gotten married. Muriel, though, had sent my pa an 8 by 10 picture. He put her picture up on the back bar, and before he died, he told everyone that this was the girl Earl was going to marry. Neither Muriel nor I knew about it, because we didn't think much about each other.

Well, I decided to go to Wyoming and see Muriel. When I got there, I went to her family's house. Muriel had moved out and was living with her aunt by then. She was managing a baby clothing store in downtown Cheyenne. At night I would stay at her folks house, and if it was too late when I came in, her dad would put a chair by the back door. When I opened it, I would knock the chair down the basement stairs and wake him up. That way he always knew what time I got in. Once he said to me, "Came in a little late, didn't you?"

We started playing checkers again, but this time he couldn't beat me. I didn't even have to smoke a cigar. Sid from Red River, Kentucky, taught me pretty good. Muriel's dad finally gave up trying to beat me, so we would play cards instead.

One night when I was in Cheyenne I took Muriel and her aunt out for dinner and dancing. (Muriel's aunt's husband wasn't home from the service yet.) We went downtown in Cheyenne to the Valencia. It was supposed to be a tie-and-suit nightclub. I had a sports jacket and slacks on, but no tie, when we went in and sat down. When the waitress came over to take our order for a drink, she said she couldn't serve us because I didn't have a tie. I said that we didn't intend on leaving, so she went and got a male waiter. He said that if we didn't leave, he would have the bouncer put us out. That got me a little upset, so I told him to go get the boss. His boss finally came over. I explained to him that I had just gotten back from overseas and that I had enough tie-wearing in the service. I told him that as far as his bouncers were concerned, they may put me out, but they were going to have some fun trying. They had a little conference and decided that we could stay, so we had a good time dancing after we had eaten. The tie rule was lifted after that.

I proposed to Muriel while I was there in Cheyenne, and she accepted. We told her folks, and they weren't opposed to it, but they wanted a June wedding on Muriel's birthday in Cheyenne. I didn't care for a big wedding, but I agreed at the time. I caught the bus after a week and went back to Wisconsin.

When I got back home, it was still colder then a polar bear's instep, and the bar business was really slow. One night it was about twenty below zero out and George B., the guy who used to beat me at checkers all the time, and Tony, a lumberjack and good friend, were at our place. The tavern had eight rooms upstairs, and downstairs beside the bar was a good-sized dining room, living room, kitchen, and woodshed. Anyway, that night just the three of us were there. I said, "Hey, George, how about a game of checkers for a drink?" George said, "How about a glass of wine and include Tony in on the drink?"

I agreed. George thought he was going to get a better free drink since he usually only drank beer at five cents a glass while wine was twenty cents. He was little on the tight side, but Tony wasn't tight with his money.

Anyway, we played three games and he lost all three. Tony was laying into him and laughing, and saying, "What's the matter, George?" George was so pissed that he walked outside in twenty below weather. He didn't say a word. About twenty minutes later he came back in and lay the money on the bar for Tony's and my drinks. He didn't have anything for himself and left. That was the last time he played checkers with me.

A part of my body was getting pretty stiff having to wait until June, so I called Muriel to see if she would come to Wisconsin to get married. It took quite a bit of talking because she didn't want to upset her folks. She finally agreed, and I sent her the money. Muriel didn't have any money left from her check because she was helping her aunt and her folks with their bills. While trying to convince her to come to Wisconsin, I don't think she realized how small the town I lived in was, I guess. She thought it was the size of Cheyenne, and over the phone she asked "Will you meet me in a taxi?" I said sure (I would say anything to get her to Wisconsin). She said it would take about a week to quit her job and get things squared away.

We didn't have a phone. The nearest phone was at the Palace of Mirrors Hotel or down at the grocery store, but the hotel was the closest. The bus she was coming in on would be on April around 6:00 P.M. By this time a few more guys had come home from the service, but in the back of my mind I kept thinking, Where am I going to get a taxi in a town of only about one hundred people?

The day before Muriel was supposed to arrive, Kelly, C.J., Hermie, Aldey, and I were in the bar celebrating a little and thinking up a welcome for Muriel.

While we were thinking, we started shaking dice. We would put one dice in a dice box, and each would get one shake. If an ace came up, he would name the drink. We would continue by passing the dice box to the next guy, who would try to shake an ace. The third guy who shook a ace had to pay. It was going too slow, so we decided to have the first one to shake an ace pay for it, but we all would have to drink. We even looked in the mixed-drink book for varieties. Needless to say, we all got loaded. I had to go to the bathroom which was still the good old-fashioned outhouse. When I came back in, I had a big scratch above my eye. It was bleeding good. Kelly asked me "What the hell happened to you?" I told him that the pee trough came up to meet me. They all got a laugh out of that. Later that evening with the help of my younger sister and a couple of local gals, we decided to dress Shorty and my sister up like Indians. Leta was supposed to be pregnant. I asked Aldey, "How about your Model A for a cab to pick up Muriel? It's a four-door, and we can paint it up like a cab."

Since the bus stop was at an intersection only a 100 feet away, we would have to figure out a route to take so she would think she was really going somewhere. We decided to go out to Water Power Resort, have a beer or two, and then come back through the woods by an old logging road. The county road to Water Power was gravel, and the logging road was just a trail road. After planning all of this, I got to thinking that with Shorty and my sister dressed like Indians (you weren't allowed to serve Indians any drinks at Water Power Resort) that they wouldn't get served a drink. So Aldy and I snuck off to Water Power to ask Mrs. McGowan if, when we came out the next night, she would say she couldn't serve Indians. She asked, "What do you mean?" and we said she would find out when we got there.

The next day around noon, we were all together trying to get things set up. Shorty and I got some whitewash to paint the Model A, and on the doors, we painted SHORTY'S AND ALDEY'S CAB—DEY AND MIGHT SERVICE. On the hood, we painted PH DAVENPORT 002 SHORT. Well that took a little while to do, and we were admiring our work when a liquor dealer drove up and asked what we were doing. We explained the deal, and he thought it was pretty funny.

After ordering our whiskey, he was hanging around buying a few drinks. I think he was trying to decide whether to go on or stay to see my new bride-to-be. It was getting to be the middle of the afternoon when we started to get Shorty ready. We gave him a bear wig and an English high hat. We put those on him and then we found a rabbit jacket for him. We also had a number one bear trap, the same one I used to set when I was fourteen years old, which we strapped onto his side. It was almost as big as he was. We also gave him an old musket-loader which was actually taller he was. Now we named him "Trapper Dan," but Trapper Dan was quite a drinker, so we took an empty whiskey bottle and filled it up with cream soda and white soda to look like whiskey. While we were doing this, another liquor dealer came in. The dealers knew each other and started talking. I made my other order with him and he started buying drinks. They decided they didn't have anything that couldn't wait until another day, so they asked if we had a couple of extra rooms. We did, so they stayed the night because they wanted to see Muriel. They both laid a twenty dollar bill on the bar and said, "Let's drink up. Let us know when that money is gone." Susie, my sister, was getting her darker makeup on. Shorty was dark enough so he didn't need any. Then Susie put my G.I. underwear on as well as my G.I. shoes. When we got in the taxi, she would be smoking a cigar. She would say she was Trapper Dan's wife. Leta had my mother's coat on with a pillow tied up in it like she was pregnant. She also had an umbrella she was going to carry.

By now the word was out that there were free drinks at Diemel's. Everyone in town also knew that Earl's new bride would be arriving at 6:00 P.M. The other two taverns were also filling up with people who came to watch the fun. There were around thirty people in our little bar having a ball. Of course, the drinks went from five cents for a glass of beer to fifteen cents for a schooner. Top shelf whiskey was thirty-five cents a shot. Anything else was fifteen to twenty-five cents a shot.

On the way Muriel was talking to the bus driver saying that she had never been to northern Wisconsin and she was going to meet me to get married. But when the bus driver pulled into Summit Lake and saw all the people looking out all the windows, he said that maybe she shouldn't get off because it was the wrong town.

Our "cab" pulled in right behind the bus. When the bus driver was getting Muriel's footlocker out, he looked at the cab and scratched his head. Of course, I was there to welcome Muriel.

I asked the cab driver, Aldey, if he could take us home. He said he had one more stop to make. Aldey had just gotten out of the navy, so he had his navy-blue tops, his white pants, and an old truck-driver's cap on. Aldey was about six foot four and weighed around 260 pounds. As we were getting in the cab, Muriel asked "What about my footlocker and luggage?" I looked over at Phil, Kelly's dad, and he said he would take care of it. There were about four or five other people at the bus stop to greet Muriel.

Anyway, when Muriel and I got in the back seat of the Model A I whispered to her that the people in the front were Indians and that it was Trapper Dan and his wife. Shorty had that bear wig, the English high hat, and the musket-loader in the front seat. My sister sat there with him smoking a cigar with my G.I. blanket wrapped around her. Muriel saw the cut on my forehead and asked me what happened. I told her it was a long story. About that time, Shorty took that whiskey bottle filled with soda and tipped it up. He drank abut a quarter of it in one swallow. Muriel's eyes got big because she had never seen anything like it. Her family didn't believe in drinking.

Well, Aldey pulled out, going down to the store where Leta was waiting with Ma's coat on and the pillow underneath. She had the umbrella open. When she got in the back seat with us, she didn't take the umbrella down outside, she took it down inside. Everyone was ducking to keep from getting poked with it. I was protecting Muriel when she whispered to me, "Honey, are all the people around here crazy?"

I said, "Just about." then I explained that we would be going on a country road with a few mud puddles, bumps, and holes. It was getting pretty dark, so she couldn't see. She didn't say much.

When we got to Water Power Resort, someone said we may as well go in and have a drink. Well when we went in, Muriel saw the bear trap strapped to Shorty. Then she saw Susie with my G.I. underwear and G.I. shoes on. She looked at them, then me, then Aldey with his navy blues and whites and the truck-driver cap. She watched Leta strutting around with that pillow under her coat. I think Muriel was too scared to say anything.

Then Shorty got up on a bar stool and put down some money, asking for a "shorty," a local seven-ounce bottle of beer. My sister sat on the floor, crossed her legs, and said, "Ug!" The rest of us sat on a stool and ordered shorties as well. Mrs. McGowan served us all a beer except Shorty and Susie, but she took his money to pay for the drinks.

When she gave him his change, she said, "Sorry, we can't serve Indians."

Shorty looked around, and Susie didn't know what to say. Shorty was stuttering, but he didn't know what to say either. He knew he been had, but he couldn't do anything about it. He and Susie both took it in stride because they didn't want to spoil the game.

We finally headed back for town on this old logging road. We were afraid the Model A would run out of gas and we would have to walk the rest of the way through the mud, but it chugged through. When we got to the tavern, the first ones to greet Muriel were the liquor dealers, and they had to have a kiss. Then some of the older people were greeting her. Then Phil (Kelly's dad) came up to Muriel and introduced himself. He said he was the local health officer and that Artie was his assistant. Phil really was a health officer. He worked for Kraft Gardens, a summer home for the Kraft Cheese bunch. But in our township, there wasn't much to do as a health officer. His assistant, Artie, was a gandy dancer on the railroad. He had his bib overalls on with his standard blue work shirt. He was also wearing his hard-toe shoes. Phil said he had to inspect all the new women coming into town, and he asked her to step over in the corner, and take off all her clothes, and he and Artie would inspect her. Muriel hollered, "Honey! Come here!" She explained to me what they wanted to do. I said that they were the health officers and there wasn't anything I could do about it. She was looking so scared that I told her that they were just B.S.ing her.

Then people were asking her questions about Wyoming and how the trip was, etc. She asked me where Susie was because she hadn't met her yet. Susie was still trying to get the Indian make-up off and change clothes, so she met Lil, Shorty's wife, and my other sister, the one with the broken leg, first.

The party went on for quite a while. Susie finally came in looking normal, and she showed Muriel her room. The next morning after breakfast, the two liquor dealers wanted to know what day the wedding was going to be because they wanted to be here. I said that I would let them know and keep a room for them. We decided on April 14, a Sunday morning, at 10:00 A.M., one hour before church service. Susie and Kelly stood up for us at the church. But that was still two weeks away.

I had to get Muriel an engagement and wedding ring but I didn't want her along so I could surprise her. So I told her that Shorty and I had to go to the ranger station to get a couple of horses to ride fire patrol. I told her we had to ride the high ranges looking for smoke. I don't remember whose car we borrowed to go to Antigo, but after we left, Lil asked Muriel where we had gone. Muriel told her what I had said, and Lil was pissed. She said. "Those two lied to you. They are going somewhere to get drunk." So Lil and Muriel decided to get even. They started drinking Ma's homemade dandelion wine. They had gotten pretty loaded by the time Shorty and I got back. I took over tending bar from Susie. Lil and Muriel were parked on a bar stool. They had drunk all the homemade wine, so they said that now they wanted some Virginia Dare.

I poured them each a glass and started to put the bottle back when Muriel said, "Give me that bottle. We paid for it." She and Lil were sillier than hell. Later that evening, Muriel said she thought she was getting sick, so I took her out on a side porch to get some fresh air. She just leaned over the rail and let it go. She said, "Boy am I sick." I started laughing. Then she kept saying, "I am going to die and it ain't funny." She finally got well enough to go to bed. When she got up the next morning, I asked her if she wanted a glass of Virginia Dare and she almost got sick again.

The oil-burning heaters we had weren't burning right, so I took a plate off the chimney. It was so full of soot that I decided to clean the chimneys. Someone told me that all I had to do was put a chain in the sack and let it down the chimney with a rope, then take out the clean-out drawer at the bottom of the chimney. Our building was so high that there wasn't a ladder in town long enough, so I figured if I could get a rope over the top, I would use some of my army training to climb to the roof. I found a rope about one inch in diameter. After a few tries, I got it over the top and secured it. It took me two tries to get over the eaves, and when I got up on the roof, I had a kid named Rolly help me. On another rope, he sent up the gunnysack and chain. Before I went up on the roof, I explained to Rolly not to take the clean-out pan out until I hollered down the chimney that it was okay. Then he could carefully shovel out the rest with the old, stove-ash shovel. He had to squeeze himself in behind the kitchen cookstove and stand on a little stool to get to where the clean out pan was. I guess Rolly thought it was taking too long, so he pulled out the clean-out pan just about the same time I was letting the chain in the gunnysack down. Since I had never done this before, I probably let it down too fast. As the sack went down, I heard some screaming. It was Ma and Muriel. They were cooking dinner for some of the men who worked in the sawmill and they also were washing and doing the ironing for the eight rooms. The soot went all over the kitchen, the dining room, and into the storage room. Rolly came running out and looked up at me. All I could see were the whites of his eyes. He asked, "What happened?" He looked so funny I had to laugh. Then Muriel and Ma came out but they weren't so nice about it. Just then, a couple of beer delivery men drove up. They saw what happened. They started cussing me, too. So I told them all that if any of them wanted me, they would have to come up and get me because I wasn't coming down. It was only an hour before the men were coming for dinner, and all the food on the stove had not been covered. It all had to be replaced. They also had to redo all the washing which meant the water had to be pumped and heated on the stove. I did finally come down to help.

The soot from the oil burners couldn't be washed off, so we had to vacuum everything. It took me about two weeks before we got most of it. And I guess you know I was pumping water like mad. About three days later, I worked on the next chimney, but I had to use the rope to get on the roof again.

About a week after Muriel arrived, the smelt were running over at Marinette, Wisconsin, so Aldey and Shorty wanted me to go with them to get some. I told them that I had better not go with Muriel there, so Aldey, Shorty, and Hermie went. When they got to Marinette, they wanted to stay at the Marinette Hotel, but they couldn't find a parking space. They circled the block, came back around, and saw a sign "Taxis Only." They said, "Hell we have a taxi," so they pulled in and parked. (That old Model A was still painted like a taxi.) They got a room where they could look out and see the cab. They said the people would walk by, point, and laugh. The other cab drivers would scratch their heads and laugh, too. Even the cops thought it was pretty funny. Well Shorty's and Aldey's cab sat there all night. No one bothered it or towed it away. They got a bunch of smelt and came home. They all got a kick out of parking in a "cab only" space and loved telling the story.

Finally the big day arrive. It was April 14, 1946, at Deerbrook, Wisconsin, at 10:00 A.M. when the Lutheran minister performed the wedding ceremony. Susie and Kelly stood up with us. Then we went on a big honeymoon over to Mountain, Wisconsin, to Shorty's folks, who also had a bar and restaurant. They fixed up a nice private dinner for the six of us. They served me a raw egg in a beer with oysters so I could make it through the night.

When we got back to Summit Lake, Ma was waiting for us. She came to the car and said that the men were in the living room and the women were in the kitchen. So I went into the living room from the outside door and Muriel went into the kitchen. It was a set-up, though, because the women were in the living room and the men were in the kitchen. There was more kissing going on than barrel of monkeys. The two liquor dealers had been there since morning, as well as buddies from Milwaukee and Chicago and all the locals. No one was feeling any pain. Then they had to have an old-fashioned shiveree with old wash boards, pots, spoons, bugle, drums. They followed Muriel and me behind the bar. After it quieted down, I said, "Free beer." I had two half-barrels of beer ready to go.

Jimmy McCoy was a top violin player, and Nova, from Chicago, was a good organ and piano player. They played on our old organ and pa's violin. Muriel and I had to have the first dance. With all the people there, there wasn't much room to dance but the music was good.

When we were ready to go to bed around 2:30 A.M., Muriel didn't want to go get undressed in front of me. She had Susie take out the light bulb for her. We had a free-standing closet in our room which stood about three feet square with a door on it. Muriel figured that with one door closed and the other door open, she could and get behind it so I wouldn't see her. She had a beautiful shape, but she was very shy. We went into our room and I pulled on the string, but no light. I said, "What the hell?"

Muriel said "Maybe it's burnt out." With the dim light from the street light near our window, I could see there wasn't a light bulb. So I thought, Oh well, we don't need a light anyway. When I went to sit on the bed to take off my shoes and clothes, I heard a big crunch. Muriel asked, "What was that?"

I said, "Those S.O.B.s." Under the blanket but on top of the sheet they had put was cut-up broomstraws. Between the sheets they had put corn flakes, and under the sheet were dried beans. I started shaking everything out onto our floor. Then I tried to remake the bed in the darkness. After that was all over, I said, "Okay, honey, you can come to bed now. Here came Muriel on her hands and knees because she didn't want me to see her.

She was going crunch, crunch and saying, "Ow, ow." I had to laugh but after we got into bed everything was fine.

Early in the morning when the sun started coming up, Muriel and I started again. Muriel asked, "Oh! What is that?" Here they had put a rubber filled with water hanging off the head of the old, cast-iron bed. Again I cussed them out a little. Finally, I told Muriel that I had to go down and get things cleaned up in the bar. Ma had to get the boarders' breakfast early so they could go to work, but we would share a later breakfast with all out company. Muriel said she would clean up the room. In the bar, we had to wash the glasses. We heated water and put it in one tank. Then we had two others for rising with chemicals. Anyway, Ma hollered upstairs that breakfast was ready. The liquor salesmen and the two guys from Milwaukee were just waiting for Ma to call them. Muriel had her housecoat on, and she thought that if she hid the rubber under the housecoat, she could get rid of it out on the back porch, since we didn't have any plumbing. Our room at that time was right by the head of the stairs. When Ma called, Muriel came out, but so did the four guys right behind her. Everyone said good morning. As Muriel started down the stairs she was still trying to hide the rubber under her robe. It fell out and broke open as it tumbled down the stairs. The guys cracked up, but poor Muriel was so embarrassed that she wouldn't even eat the big breakfast that Ma had fixed. In fact, Muriel wouldn't even come down again until they had all left. But after that, we were pretty happy together, and after fifty-one years, we are still happily married—most of the time.

Paul Austerlitz

MERENGUE

Dominican Music and Dominican Identity

Foreword by Robert Farris Thompson

TEMPLE UNIVERSITY PRESS
PHILADELPHIA

9122

versity

in the United States of America

♾ The paper used in this publication meets the requirements of the American National Standard for Information Sciences—Permanence of Paper for Printed Library Materials, ANSI Z39.48-1984

Text design by Kate Nichols

Library of Congress Cataloging-in-Publication Data

Austerlitz, Paul, 1957–
    Merengue : Dominican music and Dominican identity /
    Paul Austerlitz ; foreword by Robert Farris Thompson.
        p.   cm.
    Includes bibliographical references (p.   ) and index.
    ISBN 1-56639-483-X (cloth : alk. paper). — ISBN 1-56639-484-8
(paper : alk. paper)
    1. Merengue (Dance).   2. Dance music—Dominican Republic—
History and criticism.   I. Title.
ML3465.A95   1996
784.18′88—dc20   96-24778

Frontispiece: Joseito Mateo, the "king of *merengue*" in the 1950s. From a Riney Records album cover; copy by Robert C. Lancefield.